GW01091299

THE NEW, THINKING ANNABEL

Annabel has to do some quick thinking when she and Kate are caught coming out of the fish and chip shop at dinner time by Mrs da Susa. Only that very morning she has had discussions with the Headmaster about her unsatisfactory record of behaviour! But when Annabel sees the book Mrs da Susa is carrying, she lights upon an original way of explaining her behaviour, with the help of Betsy-Lou, her 'trans-atlantic cousin'.

In the other two stories in this volume, Annabel tries to satisfy Kate's father that she is indeed sensible enough to go on holiday with Kate, and takes on the armed might of NATO to rescue an injured rabbit.

Here are three stories about the irrepressible Annabel in which she struggles to apply some thought to her actions – with hilarious results that every thinking reader will love.

Alan Davidson's heroine first appeared in *A Friend Like Annabel* and *Just Like Annabel*, both also published in Puffin. Married with four children and living in Dorset, Alan Davidson is also the author of the marvellously gripping story, *The Bewitching of Alison Allbright*.

Other books by Alan Davidson

ALAN DAVIDSON

*****

The new, thinking
Annabel

Puffin Books

PUFFIN BOOKS

Published by the Penguin Group
27 Wrights Lane, London W8 5TZ, England
Viking Penguin Inc., 40 West 23rd Street, New York, New York 10010, USA
Penguin Books Australia Ltd, Ringwood, Victoria, Australia
Penguin Books Canada Ltd, 2801 John Street, Markham, Ontario, Canada L3R 1B4
Penguin Books (NZ) Ltd, 182–190 Wairau Road, Auckland 10, New Zealand

Penguin Books Ltd, Registered Offices: Harmondsworth, Middlesex, England

First published by Granada Publishing 1985
Published in Viking Kestrel 1988
Published in Puffin Books 1989
1 3 5 7 9 10 8 6 4 2

Filmset in Trump Medieval
Reproduced, printed and bound in Great Britain by
Hazell Watson & Viney Limited
Member of BPCC Limited
Aylesbury, Bucks, England

Contents

*****

To W. H.
Onlie Begetter of one of these
insuing stories, together with
The dark lady
All happiness

Annabel and her Transatlantic Cousin

*****

1

It was a shock to be caught coming out of the fish and chip shop by Mrs da Susa, especially on that day of all days. Perhaps Annabel had become a little bit complacent and neglected to keep a proper look-out, though it certainly wouldn't be fair to say the same about her best friend Kate.

To leave the grounds of Lord Willoughby's school during dinner break without permission was strictly forbidden. It was one of the few school rules a breach of which the Headmaster, Mr Trimm, and the Deputy Head, Mrs da Susa, were united in regarding as serious.

Such permission was granted only in cases of genuine emergency. Vague pleas such as: 'my mother asked me to get the shopping today, Mrs da Susa, because she's got a bad leg,' were no longer enough, having too often been found suspect in the past. And certainly it would not be given for frivolous reasons such as – to take an extreme example – going to the fish and chip shop.

The encounter, then, between Annabel Fidelity Bunce and her best friend Kate Stocks, both of class 3G, on the one hand, and Mrs da Susa on the other, just outside the doorway of the *Crispy Cod* in Addendon High Street at 1.06 p.m. British Summer

Time on a term-time Tuesday was not theoretically possible. But there it was and it was a shock and an embarrassment to all concerned.

If Annabel *had* become complacent it was because this was not the first time she had been to the fish and chip shop during dinner break. She had been doing so, in fact, every school-day since the previous Tuesday with Kate, loyal friend that she was, keeping her company.

This was not because Annabel wanted to; far from it. She was very ready to explain to Kate that she was getting rather tired of fish and chips and steak pies and the rest, and would have given them up gladly if it were possible. She was doing it to uphold a principle, one so fundamental that she had declared herself ready to keep on going to the fish and chip shop every day for the rest of her school-days if necessary, rather than abandon it. Though it was not a principle which could be explained easily to Mrs da Susa.

This situation had arisen because of a difference of opinion Annabel was having with her mother over school meals. Although too complicated to go into here it will be explained fully later. It was a matter of extreme importance to her, as will be seen.

Annabel didn't at first realize who it was. She and Kate were emerging from the fish and chip shop, purchases in hand – Annabel's being two jumbo sausages and chips and Kate's a fishcake and chips – heads bent together deep in conversation, when Annabel collided with this passing woman, causing the book which the woman was reading to fall to the ground. It was as much her fault as Annabel's since she had been walking slowly along the inside edge of the pavement, totally absorbed in the book and frowning and muttering eccentrically to herself.

As Annabel, with instinctive politeness, stooped to

pick up the book, first cramming the chips she was holding into her mouth and quickly licking her hand, nothing registered other than that there was something vaguely familiar about that long, narrow, tortured face. Only as she straightened up and realized that Kate was transfixed and staring did it dawn upon her that it was the Deputy Head of Lord Willoughby's she was looking at; their very own, the one and only Mrs da Susa.

'I'm sorry about the book,' said Annabel feebly, handing it back. It was a big, fat, boring-looking book in a bright red cover and had, she noticed, a title to match: *The Growing-up Years: Behavior and Development* sub-titled: *Sixty-Three Case Histories and Analyses of Disturbed Behavior amongst Schoolchildren.* Typical da Susa reading matter. The publishers didn't know how to spell 'behaviour' either. Or maybe, come to think of it, it was an American book.

Mrs da Susa glanced at it. It was fortunate that it had neatly closed itself when falling. Fortunate, too, that it had a wipeable transparent cover for there was now a greasy thumb-print on it. She had, after all, only just bought it at no small cost at the Addendon Bookshop, where it had been on order for some weeks. She was well acquainted with the book for there was a copy in the public library which she had been accustomed to borrow for long periods, but she had long wanted one of her own in order to be able to underline key sentences, insert question and exclamation marks, make notes in the margins and all the other things she liked to do with books she particularly treasured.

Then her gaze returned to Annabel and Kate, more especially Annabel. It was a typical da Susa gaze, heavy with martyrdom. It told them that while she

3

had every right to be angry, she was not. She was simply deeply disappointed and hurt that they had let her down.

'It's difficult', she said, 'to believe my eyes. Tell me, Annabel, am I mistaken in thinking that it was only this morning that you had an appointment to discuss certain matters with Mr Trimm?'

'No – er, you are not mistaken,' mumbled Annabel.

'What were those matters? What did you discuss, exactly?'

'We discussed my – er – record of behaviour this term.'

'Which has been what? Was Mr Trimm able to sum it up in a few words?'

'Er – one was enough. Unsatisfactory.'

Mrs da Susa sighed. 'Of course, I know some of the things you've been checked for –'

Certainly she did. It was she who'd drawn up the list and given it to Mr Trimm.

' – but perhaps you'd like to remind me.'

'Oh, just things like – like forgetting to do homework . . . playing the fool and showing off in class . . . shouting in the corridor . . . that sort of thing. Nothing serious.'

'And did Mr Trimm give you any punishment?'

'He let me off with a detention. Said it was my last chance. Have to take more severe action if – if I don't pull myself together.'

Mrs da Susa closed her eyes for a moment and shook her head despairingly.

'And now here you are, hardly having closed Mr Trimm's door behind you, in trouble again. I really don't know what to say. I try to treat you as young adults. I try to understand you and you let me down. I know Mr Trimm believes I treat you too gently and there really are times when I begin to wonder if he isn't right.' The hopeless look deepened to tragic proportions. 'Yes, perhaps he's right.'

'You leave me with no alternative. The Headmaster will have to deal with this. Unless, of course,' she added, sceptically, 'you have an excuse.'

They looked down at the bags in their hands. What conceivable excuse could there be? The jumbo sausages, the fishcake and the chips were for a sick relative in hospital? They were for distribution to the poor?

'I – er – I felt depressed,' Annabel said at length. 'I came here to get away from people and be alone with my thoughts.'

It was a desperate throw, merely the first thing that came into her head and she was unable to look at Mrs da Susa as she said it. It was really nothing more than a way of filling the silence which had descended since Mrs da Susa's last remark and was by now becoming embarrassing. She kept her gaze fixed firmly upon an old chip which someone had let fall on the pavement, just by Mrs da Susa's foot. It was a particularly long chip, she observed, rather pallid and now congealing. Before long, presumably, someone would tread on it and squash it.

After a further few moments, as the silence continued, Annabel risked a furtive glance upwards to see that Mrs da Susa was now gazing steadily at her, and that the hopelessness had gone from her face to be replaced by a look of cautious interest.

It struck Annabel that by pure chance she had found a form of words which made contact with the electrical circuits in the da Susa mind, starting them charging and sparking and flashing and goodness knows what. She had stumbled upon a coded phrase which, in itself meaningless, became active when presented to the system for which it was designed. It was like chancing upon the combination of a safe, causing the door to swing abruptly open and reveal the riches inside; or a scientist boredly sending a routine radio signal off into space to be rewarded with an excited reply from distant aliens; or suddenly finding oneself in communion with a chimpanzee.

Then Mrs da Susa frowned.

'But you are not alone,' she pointed out, shrewdly. 'Kate is with you.'

Annabel changed mental gear. Having struck oil by accident, she must not allow it to gush to waste because of poor follow-up work. The original statement had been such overall nonsense that it hadn't seemed to matter if certain parts were more nonsensical than others. But apparently there were certain parameters in the da Susa mind, certain limits, as to what was acceptable nonsense and what unacceptable. These limits had to be probed and explored, rather like the game of Mastermind which she sometimes played with her father in which you make tentative moves forward with different coloured pieces then wait to see if they've brought you nearer the solution.

'Kate followed me,' she said, rapidly. 'She was worried about me, weren't you, Kate?'

'Yes?' said Mrs da Susa, not ungently but with eyes narrowed sceptically, to show that she wasn't the sort to be easily fooled.

'She came out of school to find me — risked being caught and punished —' Was that going too far?

Annabel started winking and grimacing at Mrs da Susa. Kate, who had so far remained a hypnotized bystander, almost ignored because she hadn't had a discussion with Mr Trimm that morning, was

6

momentarily startled then realized that she was trying to look on the verge of tears and mildly succeeding.

Mrs da Susa turned to Kate. 'Is this true, Kate? Did you really follow Annabel because you were worried about her? Now come along. I know you're a truthful girl.'

Kate did a mental eye-roll. 'Yes, Mrs da Susa,' she replied, loyally.

This was, in fact, perfectly true. Kate *had* been worried about Annabel, worried about her breaking a school rule for the sixth day in succession and on this occasion straight after her interview with Mr Trimm; worried about the possible consequences. She had indeed suggested as much to Annabel but her observations had been brushed aside, Annabel reminding her crisply that she was not doing this for pleasure but for principle, and saying Kate mustn't come if she were worried about it.

Mrs da Susa was frowning. Her interest had been caught but she was not yet entirely convinced.

'Tell me, these worries – are they private? Or can you say something about them? Were you, perhaps, worried by what Mr Trimm said to you this morning?'

'Well, yes –' Annabel began eagerly, for a moment believing herself to be presented with an easy opening. Then she paused. It was complicated. She would need to work this one out before committing herself. It would be easy to blunder.

Supposing she were to convince Mrs da Susa that in fact the interview was the cause of her worries. *Ergo*, it would follow that the person directly to blame for her being here, jumbo sausages and chips in hand, during the dinner break, was the Headmaster himself. So far, so good.

If the proposition were to be put in this form, however, the logical solution would be for Mr Trimm to mend his ways, to stop criticizing her and threatening her and indeed to withdraw criticisms and threats already made. Perversely, therefore, the consequence of breaking an important school rule would be an apology from the Headmaster.

It was a tempting line of attack but would the logic be too much even for Mrs da Susa to swallow? Reluctantly, Annabel groped for a safer approach though without abandoning that one entirely.

' – Mr Trimm's words certainly did add to my depression, Mrs da Susa, but I wouldn't like to put the blame entirely on that. The – the –' she rolled the next sentence around in her mind, testing it before saying it out loud, and decided it sounded promising ' – the basic problems are a lot deeper. Aren't they, Kate?'

From the way the atmosphere suddenly lightened it was clear that lights were flashing and coins pouring out all over the da Susa mind. The sentence had been spot on. Mrs da Susa started to say something but decided against it as she was uncouthly elbowed aside by two youths in motor-cycling leathers who were stuffing chips into the small portions of their faces left uncovered by visors and scarves. Something soft and slippery which she trod on at this point proved to be the old chip which Annabel had been staring at. Mrs da Susa scuffed and scraped it off her shoe.

She then glanced about her, as if seeing her surroundings properly for the first time, noting the queue, which was now creeping out into the doorway, the aroma, which was powerful, and the placard in the window inquiring if her tummy were rumbling and suggesting that if so she should fill it with fish and chips. An expression of faint nausea appeared on her face.

'Look, why are we standing here?' she asked, briskly. 'I think we should walk back to school together.'

So much better did the atmosphere seem now that Annabel risked eating a chip, popping it into her mouth quickly as they moved away. Since Mrs da Susa didn't appear to notice, she tried another, and a furtive bite of jumbo sausage, and then started eating them at a leisurely pace. Kate, meanwhile, fell a step or two behind as they walked up the High Street and started eating hers, too.

They made a curious trio as they arrived back at Lord Willoughby's and immediately became the object of much attention and comment. It was unusual, to say the least, to see Mrs da Susa coming in through the gates at dinner break with two girls who were eating chips from newspapers while discoursing amiably with her. Most of class 3G were outside, having finished their school meals or packed lunches, and they gathered to watch.

The trio was seen to pause for a moment in the drive while Annabel scooped up the last salty and vinegary scraps from her bag and licked them from her fingers with relish before screwing bag and newspaper into a ball. Having asked Mrs da Susa to excuse her for a moment she moved towards a litter bin to dispose of it, pausing after a few steps to return and take Kate's, too.

They were all then seen by the dumbfounded watchers who included Vicky Pearce, Richard White, Damian Price, Fiona Turnbull, Miles Noggins and Justine Bird, to name but a few, to chuckle together, apparently sharing some joke which Annabel had made, possibly to do with Mrs da Susa's well-known dislike of litter. Annabel disposed of the papers, gave her fingers a final and thorough lick and then the trio, resuming their conversation, continued on their way and disappeared indoors.

The episode had been so remarkable that several of the observers, Vicky Pearce for instance, declared themselves unable to believe their own eyes and went around begging for confirmation while others, such as Richard White, came quickly to exaggerate it in retrospect and the rumour spread around Lord Willoughby's that Annabel Bunce, Kate Stocks and Mrs da Susa had been out to the fish and chip shop together and had come back all chattering and giggly and swapping chips from each other's bags.

But even if exaggerated, there were elements of truth in this. So how had Annabel done it? How had she fared on their progress back to school, managing to retrieve the situation from its nadir on first encountering Mrs da Susa outside the fish and chip shop to its comparative high point now?

2

High point perhaps but still fraught with danger. Mrs da Susa was precariously on the hook like some great conger eel but one false move and she would be off, lashing her tail around and snapping her teeth about again.

Annabel had very real cause for concern. Mr Trimm hadn't spelt out exactly what 'the more severe action' might be, but he had dropped hints reminding her that he had a number of weapons at his disposal. Of these, perhaps the most likely and certainly the most feared was the transfer to another class, probably 3M (the *Marauders* as they conceitedly liked to call themselves, or the *Muggins* as they were called by others; in the same way 3G had alternative names depending upon who was referring to them: the *Greats* and the *Goofs*).

To have to join their class would be appalling enough in itself. The real disaster, though, would be the separation from Kate. There was much to fight for.

Some quite subtle exchanges had taken place between Annabel and Mrs da Susa on the way from the fish and chip shop and Kate, walking behind, had admired Annabel's skill as, with growing confidence, she had kept Mrs da Susa on the hook, playing her deftly, easing the line and allowing her to run at times, hauling in vigorously and clinging to a rock when necessary.

The phrase about the *basic problems* being deeper had struck exactly the right note, reminding Mrs da Susa sharply and pleasurably of the counselling course she had been on a few years ago. (Though, alas, the skills she had learned there had been rusting ever since for Mr Trimm was too stick-in-the-mud to allow a system of counselling to be introduced at Lord Willoughby's. It was one of the most infuriating things about him.) It had excited her and loosened her tongue. Becoming animated, she had even hinted about the unsatisfactory nature of the relationship between Mr Trimm and herself, unaware that the relationship was already perfectly well known not only to Annabel and Kate but to the whole of Lord Willoughby's and most of Addendon as well.

She had given Annabel delicately to understand that Mr Trimm thought that she, Mrs da Susa, was an old fool for preferring to understand her pupils rather

than thrash and bully them. Whereas it was really Mr
Trimm who was the old fool because she had the sort
of *rapport* and understanding with young people
which he could never aspire to and she knew that
they didn't behave badly for the sake of it. There was
always a deep-seated reason and it was a question of
finding it. By the time they were in the Third Year
they were not children any longer but young ladies
and gentlemen.

Annabel, giving a lick to a rather tempting bit of
the chip-bag which had a fragment of chip stuck to it,
had agreed; subtly, of course, for no one was saying
outright that Mr Trimm was a disaster who should
have been sacked years ago and replaced by Mrs da
Susa, *if* such a thing were possible in a society where
an incompetent and bumbling idiot of a man is still
held to be preferable to a dedicated and far-sighted
woman.

For Annabel to have made any such outright suggestion would, of course, have been a gross imperti-
nence which Mrs da Susa would have had to deal with
severely. But there are ways — nods, sighs, helpless
shrugs, pursed lips, head-shakes and so on — of suggesting that one is not wholly in disagreement with
that which is being hinted at.

Such signs were called upon again when Mrs da
Susa, a wistful note entering her voice, went on to
hint that he was even unreasonable enough to point
to her lack of success when preferring his methods to
hers. As if there were any *possibility* of success when
he refused to back her up! Give her a free hand just
once and she'd show him. How she'd love to *show*
him!

Annabel, overcome by sympathy, absent-mindedly
started to offer her a chip before thinking better of it.

By the time they were back at school, therefore,

Mrs da Susa had somehow done most of the talking and, as had been observed, a certain *camaraderie* had been established. It had, indeed, crossed Annabel's mind that she might be going to forget about the incident.

Unfortunately not. Once inside the school Mrs da Susa remembered who she was and pulled herself together.

'Now, Annabel, I realize these problems may be private and personal but obviously I have to have some idea of what they are if it's to have any effect upon whether I report this to Mr Trimm or not. However much I may feel inclined to sympathize with you in the abstract, I do need to have some evidence, don't I? I can do nothing unless you are prepared to confide in me at least to some extent.

'I shall give you until first thing tomorrow morning to think about it. Report to me straight after Assembly. Otherwise I shall have no alternative but to inform Mr Trimm.'

She went off with her book and Kate was at last free to let her face sag. She herself appeared to have been forgotten about. Her fate was presumably bound up with Annabel's, but she wasn't much bothered about any punishment that might come her way in any case. It was Annabel who was in real trouble and who mattered. A transfer to 3M would, after all, be disastrous for both of them.

'What are you going to do, Annabel?'

Annabel, too, was easing her face into new shapes after abandoning the succession of false expressions which had occupied it since the fish and chip shop; false melancholy, false eager interest, false jocularity. After various shudders and exhalations of breath it settled now into one of genuine thoughtfulness. It wasn't, in fact, quite the expression that Kate would have expected. There was less – what was it? – less *worry* in it, more *reflection*. As was not infrequently the case, Kate had the feeling there was more behind that expression than was being revealed to her. Though it would be, if she had patience. It always was, given time.

Then Annabel became animated again.

'I've got till tomorrow morning to find something to be depressed about, haven't I?' Irritation crossed her face briefly. 'As if, Kate, I haven't enough on my mind already.'

Far and away the foremost of the things on Annabel's mind was the difference of opinion with her mother which had led to her being at the fish and chip shop in the first place.

For most of the first two years at Lord Willoughby's, Annabel and Kate had eaten the school meals quite happily. The food, they were agreed, had been quite reasonable for most of that time. During the last term of the Second Year, however, the standard had declined suddenly following staff changes in the kitchens and when their Third Year began it had become, in their opinion, still worse, indeed intolerable.

This had led to Annabel's famous – famous in the Third Year of Lord Willoughby's school, that is – Declaration of Independence. After finishing a meal described as *chilli con carne with mixed diced carrots and peas* and *semolina pudding* – she had eaten it only because she was *extremely* hungry – she had risen to her feet and wrathfully pronounced the *Bunce Doctrine*; that she would not eat another school dinner until the present staff had gone elsewhere and she had satisfactory evidence that the new crowd knew what they were doing. She had then swept dramatically from the dining-hall accompanied by Kate, who was in total agreement.

At their homes that evening, they had announced to their mothers that from now on they wanted to take packed lunches to school. Immediately, Annabel had run into an unexpected difficulty.

Kate's mother hadn't minded at all. Kate could have her hot meal in the evening with the rest of the family. Her brother Robert, who was in the Fourth Year, had already abandoned school meals in favour of packed lunches. Annabel's mother, however, had clucked and frowned and hesitated before agreeing, and then had continued to fuss.

'Now you're sure you wouldn't like a hot dinner today?' she would ask regularly before starting to make up the packed lunch in the kitchen in the mornings. She always insisted on making it herself although Annabel would have quite enjoyed doing so, if only to ensure thicker fillings in the sandwiches.

'Yes, Mum.'

'My mother was a great believer in a hot meal at midday. I *always* had a hot meal without fail.'

'I'd rather have a packed lunch.'

After a few days Annabel and Kate had come to prefer packed lunches for another reason. It meant they could go outside and sit on their favourite bench in the grounds instead of having to queue in the dining-hall.

And then suddenly, a week ago, Mrs Bunce had put her foot down. Annabel had arrived home from school and was looking in the biscuit tin to see if there was anything there worth eating when her mother, leaning back against the fridge with arms folded significantly – an attitude in which she might well have been frozen all day waiting for Annabel to return – announced that she was going to insist upon Annabel going back to hot dinners as from tomorrow.

Annabel had lost interest in the biscuit tin. 'But, Mum,' she had protested, horrified, 'I'm getting a hot meal in the evenings, anyway. Why should I need two?'

'My mother', said Mrs Bunce, 'always told me that it was too long a gap between breakfast and the evening meal to go without something hot. And no one could be healthier than my mother.'

'Oh, *Mum*. Anyway, what would Kate do? You can't make me leave her to have her packed lunch on her own.'

Even that left Mrs Bunce unmoved. So did the *Bunce Doctrine*.

'I made a solemn declaration.'

'I'm sorry, Annabel.'

In search of expert backing for her case Annabel gave up the Laurel and Hardy film on television she had been intending to watch and went off to the library instead, returning later with some statements copied out of books.

'Nutritionalists say, Mum, that the idea that hot meals are better for you than cold is an illusion. The temperature of the meal, Mum – I have it here on impeccable authority – is of psychological value only. And the psychological value of a Willers hot meal is counter-balanced, I can assure you, Mum, by the sight of the meal itself.'

And:

'Sandwiches or rolls, that is to say those made with wholemeal bread, are an excellent and nourishing food containing the essential fibres and proteins that we need. The old-fashioned idea that Nanny probably had, though not you of course, Mum, that bread was just a lot of fattening starch, is thoroughly

discountenanced by modern experts. Look, Mum –
it says it here.'

Mrs Bunce was unimpressed by stuff like that,
pronouncing it 'passing fads'. What her mother had
said to her counted for more than any of it. Next
morning she had handed Annabel her dinner money.

'I want you to have a hot meal today and from now
on. And no spending the money on chocolate and
crab paste and rolls and taking them into school
with you. I know you, Annabel. Now promise
me.'

With no way of escape Annabel had mumbled a
grudging promise and that day had made the first of
her regular journeys to the fish and chip shop.

'I've no alternative,' she had explained to Kate, who
had kept her company for the first time, eating her
sandwiches on the way. 'I can't break my promise to
Mum but neither can I go back on my public declaration that I've finished with school dinners till they
improve. Everybody who's still eating them says
they're worse than ever.

'I'm carrying out my promise to the letter, Kate. It's
a pity it means eating all that grease and salt and
vinegar but what else can I do? There's no other place
in Addendon where I can get a hot meal on the money
Mum's given me. And I will not break my promise
and disobey her however much I know I'm in the
right. That is an unshakeable principle as far as I'm
concerned, one I would go to the stake for.'

Despite her brave words, Annabel didn't like the
situation at all, Kate could tell that. And surely it was
an impossible one. She couldn't keep on going to the
fish and chip shop for ever – could she? Apart from
anything else, all that grease would make her spots
worse – wouldn't it? And she was right about there
being nowhere else you could get a hot meal for the

price except maybe in the pubs, which was hardly practical for Annabel – was it?

Anyway, now that she'd been caught by Mrs da Susa was it sensible even to go tomorrow?

'Of course I'm going tomorrow.' Annabel was indignant when Kate raised the subject as they were leaving school that afternoon. 'You can't seem to grasp that one can't compromise on principles, Kate. I don't think you ought to come, though. Anyway, you know how you get tempted into bags of chips and things and you can't afford them and it'll make you fat.'

Into what nightmarish, tangled web were Annabel's principles leading her? Kate couldn't see the end of it. But first things first. The urgent thing, the absolute priority, was to get out of the present difficulty; to find her a problem.

It wasn't easy, not the sort of problem which would appeal to Mrs da Susa, anyway. They got down to discussing it seriously while walking home along Church Lane together.

Annabel did consider telling Mrs da Susa about the school dinner situation and claiming it was that which was depressing her, but dismissed the thought as being not only risky but something which Mrs da Susa would not remotely comprehend. It was too – too *practical*.

Nor would she comprehend the other, real depressions of life; the fact of not being allowed to wear fashion shoes out of school like Justine Bird, only square-toed lace-ups which wouldn't ruin her feet; the fact of Andrew Torrance never looking at her while she was always directing dazzling smiles at him; the freckles on her shoulders, visible when swimming.

After all, Mrs da Susa wore square-toed lace-ups herself although she didn't have to. *And*, incidentally, what had good feet ever done for *her*?

'What Mrs da Susa would like, Kate, is something . . . you know, *deep* – that she can analyse . . . something she can occupy her mind with when she hasn't got any homework to mark . . . I can see *exactly* the sort of thing without quite being able to put my finger on it. Oh, Kate,' Annabel was suddenly despairing, 'even if I could think of the right thing I'd never be able to keep it up. She'd start questioning me and I'd give all the wrong answers. I need guidance.'

'What you need,' said Kate, practically, 'is some good case histories to look at. Like that book Mrs da Susa was carrying. Did you notice the title? That was all case histories.'

Annabel came to an abrupt halt. The look of despair faded.

'Sixty-three of them, Kate. And all exactly the sort of stuff that Mrs da Susa would recognize. Oh, *Kate*! Something like that would be *ideal*. I could borrow a problem from one of the case histories. I could make her problem – or his problem – mine. It'd be like sharing it with a friend. Out of sixty-three there'd be bound to be one I could identify with and then I'd know exactly what to say to Mrs da Susa . . .

'Do you think they've got that book in the library, Kate? That one would be best because Mrs da Susa would feel at home with it, too. We'd both feel at home, wouldn't we. It'd be cosy. Oh, I bet they haven't though. I just hope, I hope, I hope. Let's go straight there, Kate. As soon as I've picked up some tickets from home. I'll borrow Mum's.'

It *was* in the library. The librarian was quite impressed by the popularity of the book. Mrs da Susa had been renewing it regularly for months and no sooner was it back on the shelves than here was someone else staggering enthusiastically off with it.

In her bedroom at home, with Kate beside her, Annabel began her search through the case histories. She had been right about it being an American book but that made no difference. Problems were international, weren't they?

'How much time have you got before supper?' inquired Kate. 'This isn't one of the evenings your mother goes out, is it?'

'Not tonight, Kate. Supper's at the normal time. No hurry.'

Annabel found her soul-mate on page 267, case history number 36, and with a cry of delight pointed her out to Kate. Her name was Betsy-Lou.

3

Case history number 36 occupied almost seven pages of smallish type plus another page of notes and references and was a true-life account of the problems of Betsy-Lou (surnames and exact addresses were not given in order to preserve anonymity) aged 13 – the same as Annabel – a native of California, USA.

'It doesn't look all that easy to follow,' said Kate dubiously, casting her eye over it.

'You soon get used to it, Kate.'

Betsy-Lou [it began] was thirteen when she was taken into care. She was that particularly tragic type of case, a girl from an ostensibly normal, respectable, caring home environment ['all good so far, isn't it, Kate'] who became a delinquent. She was, in other words, of the solitary delinquent type as opposed to the social delinquent.

'I'm not sure I understand all that,' said Kate. 'It doesn't seem to make sense.'

'You don't have to follow it. And it doesn't have to make sense. But what I think it probably means is that Betsy-Lou learned how to be a delinquent by herself without any help from already-practising delinquents.'

Classically, in this case, there was a disturbed parental relationship, primarily with the female care-giver.

'She was having rows with her mum?' hazarded Kate.

'You see, Kate. You soon get the hang of it.'

Betsy-Lou came to the notice of the authorities after a gradual build-up in delinquency. Although well-adjusted with her peer group at school there was a history of having to be corrected with growing frequency for minor misdemeanors; lateness, failure to do set work, inattention and chattering in class.

'See the significance of that, Kate?'
'It could be about you.'
'Exactly. But read on.'

This developed into more overtly anti-social behaviour beginning when Betsy-Lou was noticed by an observant passing teacher eating junk food in the window seat of an eating house called *Smokey's Diner* when she was supposed to be at school. Challenged, Betsy-Lou flew into a tantrum, insulting the teacher and the school and saying the food at *Smokey's Diner* was 'no junkier than the stuff they dish out at school and at least you can taste it'.

'*You* didn't fly into a tantrum and insult the school food when Mrs da Susa caught you coming out of the fish and chip shop, did you?' reflected Kate, looking up from the book.

'That, Kate, is one of the things I have in mind when choosing Betsy-Lou as my soul-mate. If, somehow, Mrs da Susa's attention can be drawn to Betsy-Lou's case, then she might be impressed by how restrained and dignified my behaviour was in comparison, don't you think? But don't stop.'

No positive action such as a referral for counselling was taken at this stage, a fact which was later criticized. The Head Teacher, when questioned on this point, said: 'I thought she needed a good whack where it hurts but I wasn't allowed to give it to her,' an attitude for which he was rebuked.

Counselling did begin later but only when the situation was out of control. After her outburst, Betsy-Lou's behavior deteriorated rapidly through the merely foolishly outrageous to the irresponsible and destructive. She appeared at school, for instance, face covered in white talc with deep purple blusher and lipstick, an effect so startling as to frighten her teachers. At other times she appeared in comic and monster masks and other fancy dress.

More seriously, she disappeared from woodwork with a saw and was found sawing off one of the legs of the wooden horse in the gymnasium. Challenged, she said she was doing so because she didn't like either woodwork or gym and threw the leg away in a temper, breaking a window. Other misdemeanors are listed in full at the end of this report but they amounted to a sustained and escalating assault on the school, culminating in the occasion when, while she was being reprimanded for activating the fire alarm system causing the building to be evacuated, it was discovered that she had in fact set the school on fire. One classroom and the science lab were gutted.

About her reasons for this incident she was at first

evasive, initially saying that it was because she didn't like anything about school at all, then that she had seen someone doing it on television and it had looked good fun.

Counselling had proved of some help but it was now clearly not enough and she was taken into care where, under the promptings of an experienced and sympathetic analyst, the true reasons for her behavior emerged.

It appeared that her parents, though well-meaning, had given her little real affection. Her mother, in particular, spent her evenings out dancing and enjoying herself in night-clubs. Obviously aware of this and with deep-seated guilt feelings, for the parents were basically a very nice, sincere couple, they had sought to make amends by continually buying Betsy-Lou presents and giving her treats. Materially she lacked for nothing but, as Betsy-Lou herself said: 'I'd have done without any of it, given everything I had away, just for one little sign of real love from Mommy and Daddy like other kids get from their mommies and daddies.'

(The analyst frequently found the sessions with Betsy-Lou very moving and was sometimes near to tears.)

When questioned about the night-clubs, the parents were evasive, claiming that they only went to one once a year on their wedding anniversary. The truth probably lay somewhere in between and it was clear they had no conception of the unhappiness they had been causing their daughter.

It emerged that shortly before Betsy-Lou had first lost control of herself in *Smokey's Diner* she had been seriously disappointed when her mother, as a punishment for some minor misdemeanor, cancelled a school holiday trip to Venezuela which she had been looking forward to immensely.

The mother claimed afterwards that she hadn't been serious about cancelling the trip, only pretending to be in order to get Betsy-Lou to behave. Whether or

23

nor this was the case, the threat had disastrous consequences.

'That's the sort of nub of the thing,' said Annabel, as Kate started to turn a page. 'It goes on for pages but that about sums it up. You have to hand it to Betsy-Lou, don't you? She had fun. Lots and lots and lots of fun. Got a bit over-excited, setting the school on fire, but I suppose when she'd done everything else where was there left to go? Anyway, it got her some more attention.'

'What happened to her in the end? Do we know?'

'She's gone to a different school. One with less discipline and better food. And her mum's going to stay in at nights and be a better parent. Her parents can keep on buying her things but they've got to give them in a more loving way.'

'Betsy-Lou wouldn't have been lost for things to say to Mrs da Susa, would she, Annabel?'

'Makes one feel a bit small. They do everything so big in America. There's so much we can learn from them, Kate.'

'You think you've got enough? A problem that'll convince Mrs da Susa?'

'I think I've got a good chance with Betsy-Lou to inspire and guide me. Seeing how she operated gives you confidence.'

Annabel turned over a few pages quite fondly.

'I can picture her quite clearly, Kate. I quite feel I know her, that there's a sort of communion between us, linking us over the Atlantic.'

'A sort of transatlantic cousin?'

'Sort of, Kate.'

'Come and sit down, Annabel,' said Mrs da Susa next morning.

She was busy writing, apparently correcting the last of some exercise books, and she barely glanced at Annabel while nodding briefly towards a chair. This chair, Annabel saw, was the one which was normally placed opposite her, on the other side of the desk, but had now been re-positioned next to her, close by her right elbow. Why was this? Annabel wondered. She sat down and waited.

Whilst waiting she occupied her time by trying to squirm the chair backwards, for it was in much closer proximity to Mrs da Susa than she cared for. The study was a small one however – its smallness, particularly when compared with Mr Trimm's, was a constant source of annoyance to Mrs da Susa – and there wasn't really anywhere much to go. She was pressing the chair hard back into the corner when Mrs da Susa closed the last exercise book and placed it on the pile, laid down her pen and looked round at Annabel. Suddenly Mrs da Susa smiled, making Annabel jump.

Whilst Annabel was recovering from that, Mrs da Susa opened a desk drawer and took from it a spectacle case which she then tried to open, with some difficulty for the hinges were very stiff. After fighting with it for a time she managed to take out the glasses and put them on, fiddling with them and tapping them until they were securely positioned.

Annabel watched this in some surprise for she had never seen Mrs da Susa wear glasses before. However, having nothing better to do for the moment than analyse the analyst – for Mrs da Susa was poking about in the drawer again – she soon surmised the reason. Mrs da Susa was trying to establish the correct relationship for the interview. By her smile she was showing herslf to be a friend; by donning the spectacles, a wise friend. But did she herself realize what she was doing or was it subconscious? Interesting.

Mrs da Susa had now found out what she was looking for. It proved to be a bar of milk chocolate.

'Would you care for a piece of this before you begin?' she smiled.

'Thank you, Mrs da Susa.'

Mrs da Susa broke it in two, giving half to Annabel and laying the other half on the desk in front of her, presumably for her own use.

By this, Annabel supposed as she took the chocolate gratefully, the wise friend was showing herself to be trustworthy. This must be the sharing food thing. Primitive people sat around in jungle clearings offering each other food in order to establish trust, so that's what she and Mrs da Susa were doing. Or Mrs da Susa was, anyway. Very well. On the strength of Mrs da Susa's chocolate she was quite prepared to trust her. Though since she had brought nothing to offer in return, how did Mrs da Susa know that *she* could trust Annabel? Had Mrs da Susa thought of that?

Anyway, Mrs da Susa looked as if she were enjoying herself, which was nice. She was probably starved of all this sort of thing, analysing and counselling and nosy-parking into other people's business and so on; all the things she'd probably learned at training college – they must teach *something* there – and all the other courses she seemed to have been on; all wasted because Mr Trimm wouldn't move into the twentieth century. It must be *very* frustrating.

As for Annabel herself, she was finding it distinctly advantageous so far to be a depressed delinquent. While the rest of 3G were settling down to French she was sitting eating chocolate and being smiled at by

Mrs da Susa. She felt she wanted to show her appreciation by smiling back but Mrs da Susa was now, having closed her drawer, engaged in tidying her desk, moving some newspapers and a book which was lying open to one side to clear a space for her elbow: the *Guardian*, *Times Educational Supplement*, *Practical Fishkeeping* – that must be for Mr da Susa, he must have a new hobby – and the book – why! wasn't it? – yes, certainly the size of it and that familiar bright red cover proclaimed it to be none other than that her old friend *The Growing-up Years*: *Behavior and Development etc.* Mrs da Susa must have been reading it at her desk.

By craning her neck slightly, Annabel was able to see roughly at what point in the book Mrs da Susa had stopped reading. It looked to be at around Betsy-Lou, perhaps a little after. What a marvellous bonus it would be if she'd just been studying Betsy-Lou!

Having turned her chair a little, rested an elbow on the space she had cleared and crossed one leg over the other, Mrs da Susa got down to business.

'You understand, Annabel, I do not wish to pry into your private life. I am not asking you to reveal personal matters . . .'

'I realize that, Mrs da Susa.'

'. . . unless, of course, there is anything you particularly want to tell me in which case you can rely utterly upon my discretion.'

'Thank you.'

'But, of course, I must have some hint –'

Mrs da Susa paused, having looked Annabel full in the face for the first time.

'Annabel, what's that on your face?'

'Er – is there anything on it, Mrs da Susa. I didn't think there was.'

'It's most peculiar – a very strange colour. It looks

like – like talc and – is it lipstick? – a mixture – smeared all over it . . . !'

This was exactly what it was. On the previous evening, inspired by Betsy-Lou, Annabel had been full of cheerful plans as to how she was going to deal with Mrs da Susa. It had all looked so easy and in the morning she had delved into her stocks of make-up – mostly other people's throw-outs – and produced a lipstick discarded by her mother because it had been a bad buy, being an exceptionally gruesome bluish-purple colour. It was the nearest thing she had to Betsy-Lou's purple-black and she had applied it to lips and cheeks – lightly for she wanted to be subtle about this – with a layer of talc over the rest of her face. She had then sneaked out of the door calling 'Bye, Mum' with her face turned sharply to one side just in case her mother should catch sight of her. It had all seemed so obvious.

'Of course it's obvious,' she had insisted when Kate had anxiously queried this. 'It's going to draw Mrs da Susa's attention to the similarity between my case and Betsy-Lou's.'

Half-way to school it had seemed less obvious and on arrival not obvious at all. It had seemed silly and would probably get her into more trouble. She had dashed into the wash-basins before Assembly to clean it off. It had all been very hurried with only a few moments to spare, and the soap dispenser had almost run out, but a lot had come off on the towel and she thought she'd managed it. Apparently not.

Mrs da Susa was thrown into a dilemma by this though only momentarily. Clearly there was make-up on Annabel's face and although she herself wasn't quite sure how she felt about its use, it was certainly against school rules and she ought perhaps to be firm. However, she was now acting as counsellor rather than teacher and the first rule of counselling was that you must accept your client, which Annabel now was, without judging. A relationship having been built up with smiles, spectacles and chocolate, it was no use destroying it with criticism.

That dilemma quickly resolved, Mrs da Susa was able to consider why it was that the remnants of Annabel's make-up had struck such an immediate chord in her mind; that combination of deathly white and bluish-purple ... of course! One of the cases in the book! She had been particularly struck by it ...

Annabel was dabbing apologetically at her face with her handkerchief.

'I should wash it off later if I were you, Annabel,' smiled Mrs da Susa. She was leaning forward slightly, eyeing Annabel keenly. 'It doesn't look very nice as it is, honestly.'

Annabel stopped bothering to dab. Judging by the warmth of the smile, it hadn't been silly to put the make-up on after all. Even the remnants of it, far from getting her into trouble, were paying dividends. It reinforced her confidence in herself and in Betsy-Lou. And now what was Mrs da Susa saying so probingly?

'Putting make-up on in the mornings is rather unusual, Annabel. Did you have some reason for it?'

'I – er – I just felt like it.'

Mrs da Susa's training had taught her that when counselling the counsellor should not only listen to what the client was saying. The counsellor should also be watching for the emotions behind the words, any paling of the cheeks, clenching of the hands, lowering of eyes, general shiftiness or squirming which might betray better than the words themselves what the client was really thinking.

Annabel was exhibiting several of these symptoms now. Sensing that she was on the track of something Mrs da Susa pressed rapidly on.

'Just *felt* like it? But why? Because of . . . annoyance, perhaps . . . even *anger* against someone? You wanted to *show* someone?'

'It – it could be.'

'With whom? Surely not me!' Mrs da Susa laughed, a warm, tinkling laugh; at least, that was her impression of it. She knew she was on the right lines now because Annabel was showing *all* the symptoms, clenching her hands and looking shifty, everything. Oh, the exhilaration of counselling, of tracking down the source of a problem even when the client herself didn't know what it was, of helping others out of one's greater resources of wisdom, experience and training!

'If only', mumbled Annabel, 'Mum didn't go out so much.'

So there it was! The old classic. Mother. She might have known, indeed she had had an inkling of it the moment she had cast her mind back to that case history, Betsy-Lou, wasn't it? How very valuable those case histories were! And how predictable human actions and emotions, especially at Annabel's age! How they ran to a pattern! They all thought their problems were unique but they were age-old . . . Mrs da Susa leaned back in her chair with a feeling of well-being.

'I cannot, of course, and would have no wish to pry into your family's private affairs.' Annabel heard this with considerable relief. The strain of playing this game was already causing her to display all those symptoms of shiftiness which Mrs da Susa had been observing and she didn't want matters to become any more complicated than was absolutely necessary.

'However, Annabel, may I just ask you for about how long you have had the feelings you spoke of?'

'Oh, about –' Annabel considered the matter '– well, I suppose it's been *worst* for about two or three months now.'

'Two or three months.' Mrs da Susa eased her glasses and pondered. 'Again, you don't have to answer this unless you want to, Annabel, but remember I am here to help. When you put the make-up on was it simply as a reaction against the general depression you've felt or was it because of something specific happening to increase this depression?'

She was asking if Annabel had had a row with her mum. Annabel hung her head and produced her trump card.

'I suppose', she said, 'it was a bit annoying when Mum said she was going to cancel my new bedroom furniture. I was going to get a nice new divan and wardrobe but then Mum got angry because I was late for supper and she started criticizing me again and . . .'

She allowed the sentence to peter out because there was nothing further to say without risking exposing its total hollowness. It had taken her some time to work that one out. Unlike Betsy-Lou, she had had no trip to Venezuela or anywhere else in the offing but there had been the threat about the bedroom furniture – a mildly casual, half-hearted threat made several days ago and almost instantly forgotten – but in any case it wouldn't have been wise to have had everything *exactly* like Betsy-Lou, just near enough. Mrs da Susa wasn't as daft as *all* that.

It was clear to her that it had had the required effect, though, for Mrs da Susa wasn't the only one watching for emotions behind words. From beneath her lowered lashes, Annabel was able to keep an eye on the faster breathing, narrowing eyes and clenching hands of her partner in this interview. She was pleased, too, by Mrs da Susa's earlier reference to being 'here to help'. That was a much better reason for being here than the one she'd started out with. Things were looking good. Things were looking *extremely* good. And now Mrs da Susa was speaking gently.

'Do you sometimes, Annabel, feel that you come in for an awful lot of criticism?'

'I don't complain,' said Annabel, staunchly, 'except when it gets too much.'

Mrs da Susa was taking her spectacles off, the expression on her face so tragically pitying that Annabel wondered if they were misting up. The interview was coming to an end. Things were looking so extraordinarily good that Annabel couldn't resist trying a finishing touch.

'It's not that Mum and Dad aren't very good to me. They give me lots of things. But I'd give the whole lot away if – if –'

The words stuck in her throat. She couldn't manage them but it didn't matter. Goodwill and sympathy were hung around Mrs da Susa in an aura. She was folding the glasses and returning them to their case. Her voice was soothing, reassuring.

'I'd try to put this out of your mind for the moment, Annabel.'

'Yes, Mrs da Susa.'

The fish and chip shop incident was surely closed. Annabel rose.

'Just one more thing, Annabel. It is, of course, Third Year Parents' Evening tonight so I'll be seeing your mother later on; your father, too, I expect. Do you have any objection to my broaching this with them? Just very briefly? You know you can rely upon me to be discreet.'

Somehow, Annabel kept her expression steady, not revealing the earthquake tremor that had erupted behind it. Then suddenly it was all right again. The convulsion was over as quickly as it had come.

'Of course I don't mind, Mrs da Susa.'

She left in an atmosphere of mutual cordiality and, after washing off the rest of the make-up, made her way to French, entering the classroom with the air of one who has been attending to more important business. Sitting down beside Kate, she responded to her anxiously inquiring look with an airy little wiggle of the hand to show that everything had gone absolutely swimmingly. Her manner would have told Kate that, anyway.

Mrs da Susa, meanwhile, had drawn her book back in front of her and was refreshing her memory with the details of the Betsy-Lou case. The parallels were truly remarkable.

What a tragedy it was that there had to be some misdemeanour before she was able to lift a corner of the curtain that hid her pupils' lives from her, and perhaps do something to help. The modern school was, after all, not merely an educational forcing house but about equipping the pupil for life, something Mr Trimm could not seem to understand.

No one could be more hard-headed than she was and she had been prepared for wild excuses, but instead she had been impressed by the quietly understated way in which Annabel had conveyed her problem; a problem which could hardly be other than genuine in its classic simplicity: a feeling, no doubt misguided, of lack of mother love. If she had had any doubts at all they would have been removed by the frank, open manner in which Annabel had consented to her raising the subject with her parents.

What to do now, though? Would it be enough merely to let the matter drop, providing of course that Annabel promised not to transgress again? Or would that be evading her responsibilities? Now that she had inadvertently become involved shouldn't she be taking a more positive interest in the problem and trying to help? After all, problems escalated. Betsy-Lou's certainly had. Now what was it that had happened there?

Mrs da Susa reminded herself. Doing so, her frown deepened, steadily at first, then sharply.

4

'No, I'm not worried about Mrs da Susa meeting Mum and Dad tonight, Kate –'

'But, Annabel! They'll blow the whole thing!'

'– because they won't be there. They don't know it's Parents' Evening. I didn't give them the note.'

'Oh!'

'I didn't want them to be worried, Kate. Mum and Dad have enough on their plates without feeling they have to come to Willers and listen to all that grumbling and nagging. It only depresses them. It's turned out for the best, though, hasn't it?'

French was over. They were sauntering to biology and Annabel was luxuriating in her successful handling of the interview. Kate still couldn't quite believe the crisis was over.

'I'd never have done it without Betsy-Lou to inspire me. I just wish I could thank her, Kate.' Annabel became reflective for a moment and perhaps just a trifle uneasy. 'I don't think Mum would mind about me mentioning her to Mrs da Susa, would she? I mean, I said nothing that wasn't true about her and it's in such a good cause.'

They were entering the biology lab.

'A good cause? You mean saving you from getting sent to 3M?'

'Oh, *that*! I'm not sure I've ever believed Mr Trimm would send me to 3M, Kate. He hints about these things but have you ever known him *do* it?'

It took Kate's breath away. 'Well, if you're not worried–' she wasn't prepared to let Annabel get away with such airiness *quite* so easily '– what have we been getting so worked up about? What is this good cause?'

'Life isn't all about self-interest, Kate.'

Kate wasn't able to ask what she meant by that exactly because Miss Ballantyne entered the lab just then and sweetly asked them all to be quiet and sit down. Anyway, she could tell she wouldn't get a very satisfactory answer. Annabel had that slippery look about her.

And, moreover, why was she allowing herself to be lulled? Even if the present battle *had* been won, which was not absolutely sure, it remained only a battle in the long war of attrition which lay ahead as long as Annabel insisted on sticking to her principles about the fish and chip shop.

They went there again at dinner break (for Kate was, for her part, equally determined that Annabel should not have to go alone). It passed off without incident but it was nerve-racking, akin to a raid into enemy territory. Kate was beginning to think of it as 'the fish and chip shop run'.

Where, oh where, oh where, would it end?

*

At the Parents' Evening Mrs da Susa glanced around the Assembly Hall in the vain hope of seeing Mr and Mrs Bunce. She was having to soothe Richard White's parents at the time, but she was used to that and had attention to spare.

'What are you going to do about it then?' Mr White was demanding, crisply. He was a wiry, thin-faced, forthright little man. He worked for the Water Board.

'I was hoping you might be able to assist,' sighed Mrs da Susa. 'Richard's education has to be a matter of co-operation between school and home.'

It was wet outside and there was a smell of dank raincoats in the Assembly Hall. Lord Willoughby's Third Year Parents' Evening was nearing its close and people were drifting away but Mrs da Susa still had a small queue to attend to. Mr and Mrs White were seated squarely in front of her. Beyond them, Mr and Mrs Noggins sat waiting to hear the worst about Miles while behind them Mrs Channing stood tapping her foot impatiently and projecting her personality. They had already discussed her Julia in detail, but apparently she'd thought of something else.

Mr and Mrs White were looking unimpressed.

'We pay all them taxes to have Richard educated, and then you tell us all he does is lark around and not learn anything and *we're* supposed to do something about it. I got my own job to do.'

'We only have Richard for a few hours a day, Mr White. We both have our parts to play.'

'We play ours, don't we, Sue. Knows better than to come it with us, doesn't he.'

'What are you going to do about it?' asked Mrs White.

They left looking dissatisfied, to Mrs da Susa's regret. They were the only parents who took this attitude. While Mr and Mrs Noggins were moving forward she took the opportunity to look around for Mr and Mrs Bunce once again, though with little hope now.

Only a scattering of parents remained, some still deep in earnest conversation with teachers, others chatting amongst themselves. Mr Trimm prowled amongst them, hands clasped behind his back, jaw jutting menacingly as if he'd like to throw everybody out which was probably the case. As far as he was concerned, a parent's place was in the home. They got reports, didn't they? There was Kate Stocks's mother, chatting to Mr and Mrs Dill. Mr Stocks was standing alone by the door, shifting from one foot to the other as if anxious to go. But of the Bunces, there was no sign.

She had been reluctant to accept that they weren't coming but now she had to look facts in the face. She had spent some time planning exactly what she was going to say to them but, more than that, not to attend Parents' Evening was a cardinal sin in Mrs da Susa's eyes. She had no time for parents who took no interest in their child's education. If she hadn't been particularly looking out for them their absence might have gone unnoticed, but now that she came to think about it, had they attended last term's . . . ?

This really did throw into sharper focus the problem that Annabel had hinted at. Mr and Mrs Noggins were waiting for her attention but one thing was increasingly clear. The situation ought not to be left here.

There was another scare on the fish and chip shop run next day. Kate saw Mr Rogers coming out of the hardware shop in front of them carrying a rake and had to push Annabel into a doorway in case he saw them. She didn't know how much more of this she could take, though Annabel's chief concern seemed to be that she had dropped a chip.

At least there had been no further word from Mrs da Susa though and it looked as if Annabel was right about that particular crisis being over. Annabel herself certainly thought so, though she was taking the precaution of keeping out of Mrs da Susa's way. On the way home she was extremely cheerful and anxious to discuss with Kate the subject of her new bedroom furniture, which she had mentioned to Mrs da Susa. It was a very interesting subject for her mother was ready to listen to her preferences and she had to come to a decision on what they were. New – or at any rate secondhand 'new'? Or something more interesting and solid, from an auction, perhaps?

'Why', said Annabel as they prepared to separate on the corner of Badger's Close, 'don't you come and have a look at my room tonight and give me your opinion?'

Kate would have loved to but she did have a lot of homework. 'I'll ring about seven and let you know if I can,' she promised. 'Your mother wouldn't mind, would she?'

'Mum won't be there, anyway. It's one of her nights out. We're having supper early.'

For Annabel truly had not been making anything up when intimating to Mrs da Susa that her mother was going out a lot at present.

'I quite like it when Mum goes out. We can make as much noise as we want. Dad never hears anything.'

Mrs Bunce went off at a quarter to six. At five past seven the phone rang just as Annabel was finishing off her homework in the kitchen.

'That'll be Kate,' she cried to her father, dashing to the hall to take it.

'It often is,' replied Mr Bunce, not looking up from his newspaper.

'Addendon Dogs' Home,' Annabel growled jollily into the phone. 'Aunt speaking.'

There was a brief silence at the other end of the line then a disconcerted voice said, 'Aunt? Aunt who?'

'Aunt you a silly nuisance.' Annabel laughed merrily into the telephone. It was to be her last laugh for some little while.

'Look, have I got the right number?' said the voice sharply. 'Could you repeat who you are?'

There was something uneasily familiar about that voice. The trouble was that it was in the wrong context; in another place it would probably have been immediately recognizable but not here in the secure surroundings of home where it didn't belong, where it was not wanted and where one had always instinctively felt safe from it.

'Er – it's flexible who I am,' replied Annabel, startled into momentary honesty. 'Who – er – who did you want to talk to?'

'I was hoping to speak to Mrs Bunce. Is that Annabel? This is Mrs da Susa.'

Annabel resisted the impulse to slam the phone down. Instead, she paused, swallowed, and did her best to inject a depressed, downcast note into her voice without making the switch from her previous merriment too abrupt.

'Mum's out tonight, I'm afraid, Mrs da Susa,' she intoned mournfully.

'Out!' Mrs da Susa was on to the word like a terrier. 'Oh dear! I was sure you wouldn't mind me contacting her because you did agree to my speaking to her, but she didn't come to the Parents' Evening last night. I wouldn't have thought she'd forget. Your father wasn't there either. I suppose you did pass on the note – ?'

Annabel stalled for a time with a non-committal croaking noise then said virtuously: 'I wouldn't forget something like that, Mrs da Susa.'

'No, I didn't think you would. Perhaps I'll ring your mother again tomorrow evening.'

'She'll be out again, I'm afraid.'

'Again? Then perhaps –'

'She'll be out Saturday evening as well.'

There was a silence. Then Mrs da Susa said crisply: 'Thank you, Annabel.' She paused again before continuing, this time with a note of concern in her voice: 'You're not alone there, are you? Is your father at home?'

'Oh, it's all right. Dad's here.' A sudden fear of Mrs da Susa appearing on the doorstep to keep her company put urgency into Annabel's voice. 'He's very busy at the moment though . . . doing something . . .'

'Perhaps I should have a word with him . . . on second thoughts, no . . .' There was another pause and some ummings as Mrs da Susa's thought processes ticked over almost audibly. 'Try not to feel depressed, Annabel. You wouldn't care, I suppose – I don't wish to be inquisitive but – you wouldn't care to tell me where your mother is?'

'She's at the King's Head at Cogginton.'

'Is that the public house?'

'I think they call themselves a – a sort of roadhouse now.'

'I see.' The pause was very significant this time. 'Is that where she's going tomorrow night as well?'

'Yes.'

'And Saturday?'

'Yes.'

Mrs da Susa's voice was very gentle now.

'Annabel, if you ever feel you need to talk about anything, you know where I live, don't you. Napoli, in Woodland Drive. It's the third bungalow on the left with cypresses in the front garden. We planted them ourselves, you know, Annabel, to remind my husband of Italy. All you need to do is phone to give me a few minutes notice.'

'Is Kate coming round?' asked Mr Bunce as Annabel absent-mindedly wandered into the sitting-room. But she had already realized her mistake and disappeared before he'd finished the sentence. The phone began to ring again as she passed it but she was able to snatch it up before it got going properly. It was Kate. She couldn't come round, alas, because her mother was insisting she wash her hair.

But Annabel didn't feel like talking about bedroom furniture, anyway.

The following day, Friday, was a terrible one. For a start, Mrs da Susa smiled at her encouragingly in the corridor. Then there was the fish and chip shop run which even Annabel suddenly seemed to find a strain, probably because everything was collapsing round her, while Kate wondered how they could go on. Overshadowing everything, though, was the fear of Mrs da Susa's next move.

For Mrs da Susa had only to lift the phone and contact Annabel's mother at any time during the day for the worthlessness of Annabel's position to be exposed. She would learn, among other things, that Mrs Bunce was not spending three evenings a week (*three*, not every evening as she no doubt currently imagined) at the King's Head for the fun-loving, irresponsible reasons which might be supposed. She was working there for a few weeks as a part-time

41

waitress and washer-up to earn some extra money, mainly to pay for Annabel's coveted new bedroom furniture.

'Oh, what a tangled web we weave, when first we practise to deceive,' sighed a tortured Annabel at afternoon break. 'Mum's always quoting that and she's right. Do you think this'll be a lesson to me, Kate?'

'Don't suppose so.'

'I never *dreamt* she'd ring up home. It's not playing by the rules. She belongs in school.'

'Mrs da Susa's very keen on co-operation between school and home, Annabel. We should have been ready.'

'It means there's nowhere to hide.'

What would Mrs da Susa's next move be? Having telephoned Annabel's mother once was it likely she'd stop there? Surely not. The crisis hadn't ended, after all. It was just beginning.

'I've blackened Mum's name, Kate. She'll never forgive me. Mrs da Susa'll never forgive me, either.'

Now that 3M was apparently a possibility again, Annabel no longer seemed quite so airy about it. And Betsy-Lou had sunk in her estimation.

'Perhaps I got carried away by Betsy-Lou, Kate. Perhaps she made it seem too easy.'

At four o'clock, however, there had still been no word from Mrs da Susa.

'Maybe Mum and Mrs da Susa have come to an agreement,' Annabel suggested nervously on the way home. 'Mum's insisting upon striking the first blow at me and Mrs da Susa's going to have to wait till Monday for her turn.'

It was Friday. There ought to have been a luxurious, carefree, sunny, weekend-ahead-and-no-school-till-Monday feeling but that was all spoilt. Home was no longer a sanctuary. Annabel sidled in through the door prepared for the worst only to hear her mother humming happily tò herself as she made an early supper again before going off to her job.

Then Mrs da Susa obviously hadn't rung so far and probably wouldn't do so in the evening because she'd know that Mrs Bunce would be out. The load on Annabel's mind lifted a little. By ten to six when her mother had left it had lifted still further. Whatever might be going to happen, at least it didn't look as if it were going to happen immediately and that was always cheering. Her natural optimism began to surface again and by seven o'clock she was ringing Kate to tell her that they might have been panicking unnecessarily.

She also wondered if Kate would like to walk to the High Street with her. Her father wanted some orange juice for breakfast and the High Street Stores stayed open till eight.

'You know, Kate,' she said, some twenty minutes later, just after they had emerged from the High Street Stores with the orange juice and some crisps they had bought for themselves, 'I have a funny feeling, an *instinct*, that Mrs da Susa's going to forget all about it and won't bother any more.'

They were pausing on the edge of the pavement as she said that to allow passage to an elderly French car, the sort that looks as if it's been hammered together out of sheets of corrugated iron. Instead of passing, however, it slowed and stopped in front of them, slightly nearer their side of the street than the other but not much, and the passenger seat window was opened by Mrs da Susa's husband. He was grinning cheerfully and wearing what looked to be his best blue suit complemented by a bright red and yellow flowered tie with an enormous knot in it. Beyond him, another face was peering at them together with an imperiously beckoning finger.

'Annabel!' called Mrs da Susa. 'Here a moment please.' There was something conspiratorial about her.

After the first shock of horror had died down, Annabel moved reluctantly forward.

'I'm quite pleased to have seen you, Annabel. I just wanted to mention to you that my husband and I have decided to have a meal out this evening. At the *King's Head* at *Cogginton*.' She looked closely at Annabel to see if the significance of this had sunk in. It had. 'We understand they do quite a nice meal there.'

She gave a farewell nod, also significant, and turned the ignition key preparatory to moving off again, forgetting that the engine was still running anyway. There was a ghastly grating noise which she and her still-grinning husband seemed to accept as normal. Behind them, a car hooted politely.

'I've heard', Annabel called urgently above the racket, 'that the food's all heated up there. They cook it somewhere else – in America, I think – then bring it to the King's Head in packets and warm it up again. It's not very nice. It gives you indigestion.'

Mrs da Susa was too busy, now grating her gears, to hear. Mr da Susa, obviously looking forward to an evening out, didn't care. He wouldn't be paying for it anyway. He raised the window.

'They've got piped music there,' Annabel shouted desperately, face close to the window. 'Or maybe it's a juke-box. Dad hates it.'

Mr da Susa winked at her and the car gathered itself like a much-flogged but still stupidly loyal mule and strained away in the direction of the Cogginton Road.

Mrs da Susa had spent her spare moments during the day checking through her reference books, reflecting upon Annabel's problems and their possible solution and the best way to tackle Mrs Bunce. She had decided upon the bold approach, confronting her directly and perhaps shaming her at the scene of her crimes.

'At least', mumbled Annabel, distraught among the exhaust fumes, 'the waitress service will be good.'

To her father's surprise, Annabel went to bed shortly after arriving back home, saying that she felt like getting a good night's sleep. The real reason was fear. She was nervous that her mother, after meeting Mrs da Susa at the King's Head, might be so angry she'd throw off her pinafore or whatever it was she dressed up in there and come charging home.

Lying awake she tried to imagine the scene in the King's Head; the da Susas having their pre-dinner drinks, Mrs da Susa sipping her tomato juice and eyeing the women there to see which was the contemptible one amongst them who was deserting her family every evening for a good time, not caring that she was turning her daughter into a delinquent; puzzled at not seeing Mrs Bunce; perhaps accosting and insulting some innocent stranger.

That thought gave Annabel a mild flicker of hope. It was, after all, some time since Mrs da Susa had seen her mother at a Parents' Evening. Perhaps she wouldn't recognize her?

Foolish optimism! Yes she would, probably over the menu when they'd sat down for their meal and Mrs da Susa was beginning to wonder if she'd got the wrong pub. Who would recognize whom first?

Then, after the surprise of seeing Annabel's mother as a waitress, would come the getting down to business, probably conducted with some difficulty because Mrs Bunce would have to carry on serving customers. Would Mrs da Susa follow her around to question her? Would she be tactless and get hit over the head with a tray or coffee poured over her or a pudding pushed in her face? Would Mr da Susa defend his wife? Would the other customers restrain him? Perhaps, oh happy thought, the da Susas would get thrown out . . .

Alas, however it developed there would come the calming down, the sorting things out, the realization that both sides had been hoodwinked. All their fury would be turned against the real villainess . . . hate, hate, hate, hate, hate . . .

Annabel pulled the duvet over her head.

(In fact, it was Mrs Bunce who recognized Mrs da Susa initially. She came out of the kitchen carrying a tray with a customer's order on it calling 'Who's the trout?' and a woman seated with her back towards her turned her head and said: 'I am.'

'Why, Mrs da Susa! I wouldn't have expected to find you in a place like this!')

Annabel continued to lie in bed late the following morning but when her mother still hadn't stormed in at twenty to ten she decided she couldn't stay there for ever and got up to face the music. Having washed and dressed she entered the kitchen cautiously. Her mother was standing with her back towards her, deep in thought, hands resting on the edge of the sink and gazing, immobile, out of the window. She could have been there all night.

'Hello, Mum.'

Mrs Bunce didn't reply or look round. Annabel

started cutting some bread for toast. Her hand was unsteady. The washing machine gave a brief preliminary chunter than roared into sudden violent action, making her jump.

'Mrs da Susa came to the King's Head for a meal last night,' said her mother. 'With her husband. I waited on them.'

'Oh!' said Annabel. She plopped two slices of bread into the toaster.

'We had a long discussion about you.'

'Oh!' in a slightly higher pitch. Annabel switched on the toaster and went to examine the teapot closely. It was cold. She'd have to make some more.

'She's coming here to see me again this morning. We still have more to talk about. She should be here any minute.'

'*Oh!*' Two-toned this time rising from approximately contralto to falsetto.

'Annabel, what are you doing? Don't empty the tea-leaves down the sink. I don't want it blocked. Empty them in the garden.'

Annabel was thankful to escape. She opened the door to the garden and stepped outside. A car was pulling up in front of the house. She flattened her back against the wall and peered desperately along the drive at it like a film gunman preparing for a shoot-out with her teapot.

The car was Mrs da Susa's. The unthinkable, the ultimate had happened. Mrs da Susa had arrived in Badger's Close like an extra-terrestrial being. Annabel had steeled herself for the worst imaginable but not for this. It was too much. She bent low and scurried into the back garden, pausing by the *Madame Isaac Pereire* rose, her mother's favourite.

Mrs Bunce liked the tea-leaves to be emptied around its roots. She believed them to be the secret of

47

its success. Annabel dutifully tipped them there then hovered, anguished.

Mrs da Susa was at the front door now. Faintly she could hear the bell ... Putting the teapot down beneath the rose, Annabel fled to the bottom of the garden. She scrambled over the wire fence on to the Hewitts' little lawn and made her way out into Brock's Gardens by way of their drive, ducking to avoid being seen as she passed their kitchen window. A few minutes later she was sitting panting in the Stocks' kitchen. Kate's parents were out shopping.

'Oh, Kate,' she sobbed. 'I made a terrible mistake, didn't I. I thought that what Betsy-Lou could do, I could do. I forgot that everything's madder in America than it is here. You can't get away with the same things here. They're daft but not daft enough.'

'What are you going to do now, Annabel?'

'I don't know.'

Kate was sad, too. It looked like 3M after all.

Some twenty minutes later, as Annabel was mournfully sipping some tea that Kate had made for her, the telephone rang.

'It's your mother, Annabel,' Kate called, anxiously.

Annabel took the telephone with a fatalistic shrug.

'Hallo, Mum.'

'Annabel, where's the teapot?'

'Under the *Madame Isaac Pereire*.'

'I couldn't find it and Mrs da Susa would like some tea and then I remembered you'd gone off with it. You left your toast, too. You're all right are you, Annabel? You just nipped round to see Kate, did you?'

'I'm fine.'

Annabel went back to the kitchen bemused.

'Is it a trap, Kate? She sounded quite ... gentle. It must be a trap.'

At eleven o'clock Annabel decided she'd better go

back. It had to be done sometime and Mrs da Susa would surely have gone by now.

Nevertheless she reconnoitred carefully to make sure the car wasn't there before entering the house through the kitchen door.

Her mother was standing by the kitchen sink again in exactly the same attitude as before. It was as if they were making a film and the first take had been a flop, so they were having to do a second with a new script.

'Hallo, Mum.'

'Hallo, Annabel.' This was exactly as before; the calm before the storm.

'Mrs da Susa's gone, then.'

'Yes. She was sorry not to see you. Have you had some breakfast? You went off without any.'

'Kate gave me some cake.'

'Cake! You need a proper breakfast. I'll make you something. And Annabel . . .'

'Yes?'

'Sit down, would you.' She was folding her arms now, turning. This was it. 'Mrs da Susa and I have been having some very frank discussions, *very* frank. She's told me about the conversations you've had with her and there appears to have been quite a lot of misunderstandings which are all cleared up now.'

'Oh, good.'

'She's thought things over overnight and this morning she had some suggestions to make and between us we've come to a decision.'

'Yes?'

'You'll be going back to packed lunches on Monday.'

'It's one of those rare cases,' said Annabel, 'in which everyone winds up happy. You can't ask more than that, can you, Kate.'

49

It was dinner break on Monday and they were back on their favourite bench in the school grounds eating their packed lunches. The fish and chip shop run was a thing of the past.

Annabel lifted one side of a deliciously crusty roll and liked what she saw. The ham was thick and the home-made pickle her favourite; all prepared with extra care by her mother's loving hands.

'Mum's been pushing food at me all weekend,' she said. 'I can't think of a better solution to my problems.'

Mrs da Susa, keeping an eye on them as she strolled by behind them – not by chance – observed the happiness and was delighted. She was mentally composing a confidential memorandum to Mr Trimm outlining the details of Annabel's case and – she was confident – its successful outcome. Unemotionally yet with icy clarity she would point to the efficacy of her approach in a case which she had handled in her own way, without interference, and draw conclusions for the future.

How glad she was now that she had not reported Annabel to Mr Trimm for him to continue blundering about in his usual rough way. It had, after all, been straightforward enough to sort out the misunderstandings between Annabel and her mother. Clearly, Mrs Bunce had been acting for the best all along but, like the mother in the Betsy-Lou case, she simple hadn't appreciated how her behaviour might be misunderstood by a sensitive daughter.

It was pleasing, too, that the Bunces' absence from Parents' Evening had not in fact been due to lack of interest (although even without a note they *might* have remembered that one was due if they'd really tried). But, anyway, she could see *exactly* how

Annabel, resentful at being apparently shut out of her mother's life, might respond by trying to shut her out of her own.

Yes, sadly, misunderstandings were a constant and inevitable part of life. If they weren't, people with her skills wouldn't be so necessary.

But it was her recommended solution of which she was most proud. The key to the whole thing had obviously been to find a way of reassuring Annabel of her mother's continuing love. She had spent most of Friday night thinking about it without getting anywhere and then the answer had come in a flash on Saturday morning after Mrs Bunce had made a passing reference to the dispute over packed lunches. Of course! It had obviously been absolutely the wrong moment to stop them. The preparation and offering of food was very much bound up with love – think only of the birds bringing beetles to the gaping mouths of their young in the nest. They must be reinstated immediately. Keen advocate of school meals though she normally was this was a case for an exception. Annabel must be given packed lunches again; they must be made by Mrs Bunce with her own hands with as much loving care and thought as possible.

'Mrs da Susa looks very happy today,' said Kate. She had glanced round and seen Mrs da Susa heading towards the school building. 'She's talking and giggling to herself.' She looked back at Annabel. 'Anyway, are you feeling reassured?'

Kate had learned about Mrs da Susa's solution from Annabel who had elicited it from her mother with some subtle questioning.

'Very. This is a much better packed lunch than I used to get. Mum's put all sorts of interesting little things in it.'

Annabel sniffed at something chocolaty-smelling in a wrapper.

'All my problems are over, Kate, and without sacrificing my principles. It's lovely.'

'Annabel . . .'

'Yes, Kate?'

'If you really weren't worried about Mr Trimm sending you to 3M . . .'

'Yes?'

'What *were* you worried about?'

Annabel looked evasive again just for a moment, then candid. She glanced round to where Mrs da Susa was nearing the school door.

'I was concerned about Mrs da Susa.'

'About – ?'

'She so badly wanted a little triumph, Kate. Something of her own to boast about to Mr Trimm. I know how she feels. I wanted my case to be a success for her sake. Oh, I know Mrs da Susa can be a terrible nuisance, but she has her problems, too, you know.'

Mrs da Susa's back was straight and springy as she disappeared through the door.

'I owe Betsy-Lou an apology, though, don't I, Kate? I slandered her, didn't I?'

'Did you?'

'I lost my faith for just a little while. I thought perhaps she had it easy because things are madder in America but I was wrong. They're just as mad here, Kate.'

Annabel brushed some crumbs from her lap and stood up. She pointed.

"The west is where the sun sets, isn't it, Kate. That way.'

She turned her face into the soft western breeze.

'Somewhere over there is Betsy-Lou. Beyond Addendon Hill, beyond the wide Atlantic and the rolling prairies and the mighty Rockies – if my geography's correct, Kate, there she is in California by that shining blue Pacific. What's she doing now? What new trails is she blazing! Ever probing the limits of human daftness, exploring the frontiers of what she can get away with next, pushing them back for others to follow, pioneering as her forefathers before her pioneered into the wilderness in their covered wagons . . .'

Annabel straightened up and squared her shoulders. She cupped her hands round her mouth and called to the western sky.

'Betsy-Lou . . . transatlantic cousin . . . I salute you! The new world has much to teach the old. I salute and thank you, Betsy-Lou.'

And surely, soughing faintly in the breeze that whispered from Addendon Hill, came the reply.

'Annabel, you're welcome.'

Annabel tries to be sensible

*****

1

'I *am* sensible,' said Annabel, stiffly.

'I'm only telling you what Dad said, it's not that *I* don't think you are, Annabel. Obviously, it's silly but . . .' Kate's voice became a mumble. She looked very disconsolate. '. . . you know what Dad's like.'

In fact, Mr Stocks had said considerably more than Kate was passing on, some of it rather forcibly, but there didn't seem any point in being too specific. Annabel was offended enough already.

'So he's thinking of not letting me go to the seaside with you.'

'What he said was,' said Kate, carefully, 'that at the seaside there are all sorts of dangers and temptations and that it's particularly necessary to be sensible but that with . . . with a whole week on holiday you – some people might get silly. And we'd be staying with Gran and Grandad and they're not as young as they used to be and all that and they wouldn't be able to watch us all the time etcetera, etcetera . . .'

It was the dinner break and Annabel and Kate were sitting on their favourite bench in the grounds of Lord Willoughby's eating their sandwiches. Kate had been bracing herself all morning to bring up the subject of Bungthorpe.

Earlier in the year Kate's grandparents – on her father's side – had moved to a cottage at Bungthorpe on the east coast after her grandfather had retired. Annabel and Kate had been much excited by the idea of having relatives at the seaside and their hopes of an early invitation had not been disappointed. Kate had been asked if she'd like to come and stay during the second week of the school holidays and bring a friend. The friend would, of course, be Annabel. Now, with the holidays almost on them, Kate's father was, apparently, demurring.

'He's not saying he's changed his mind,' said Kate. 'Just that he's become a bit uneasy, that's all. I suppose you can understand it. I've never been away on holiday before without Mum and Dad.'

'I've been working to earn money to go,' said Annabel, indignantly.

'I know,' said Kate.

'*And* I've bought a rubber dinghy. With my own money.'

Kate shifted uneasily on the bench and looked even more miserable.

'Actually, Annabel, it was when I mentioned the rubber dinghy that . . . well, it's what sparked him off. He said they can be dangerous. Any number of people have been drowned when their dinghies drifted out to sea. He said that whether or not you come to Bungthorpe with me he'd like to make sure we can handle it properly before we go out in it alone. He suggested we – we try it out on the river with him watching . . . next Monday evening would be a good time . . .'

Annabel had become cold again.

'Oh, Annabel, it won't be any real problem. It's just Dad fussing. I wouldn't want to go to Bungthorpe either if you can't but I'm sure it'll be all right. It's just a matter of trying – well – to remember to look sensible when Dad's around.'

Colder.

'I think I'm extremely sensible,' said Annabel. 'In fact, when I look around I often think I'm the only sensible person left in the world. Apart from you, of course, Kate.'

She got up suddenly.

'*Extremely* sensible,' she repeated.

She walked back towards the school building rather more erectly than was usual and Kate followed unhappily.

'You've got to make allowances for Dad,' Kate mumbled, 'he seems a bit low just now. I think maybe he's fed up with his job or something. I've noticed him looking at the adverts in the paper lately.'

This was stretching things. It was true that Kate had seen her father looking at the job adverts but to be strictly honest it had only been on one occasion and then idly, probably in passing while looking for the sports pages.

However, she felt a need to make excuses for her father and present him in a sympathetic light in order to soothe Annabel. Mention of other people's troubles usually had the effect of making Annabel forget her own.

It worked, for Annabel's face instantly softened. In the school doorway, she paused.

'Perhaps your Dad's right, Kate,' she said. 'Perhaps I can understand his worries. I can be sensible. I *will* be sensible. I'll show him.'

She walked on again but now slowly and thoughtfully.

'Really, really sensible.'

Her features were already assembling themselves

into a sort of stern, solemn stare. Presumably the expression felt sensible.

Annabel started practising being sensible immediately, as was evident to Kate because she simply became inactive. This was because, Annabel explained between lessons that afternoon, to take any action risked being unsensible. Inaction was safe.

The truth of this was demonstrated during the last lesson of the afternoon, maths, when she did take two small actions on her own initiative and was noticed by Mr Rogers and promptly given lines for it. The actions were to write, in ballpoint pen on the back of her hand in thick, ornate letters the words BE SENSIBLE and then, feeling she could improve on that, to write in even thicker, larger letters on her knee THINK CLEARLY.

When she stood up, of course, that would appear upside down to anyone else but, muttered Annabel as she worked on it, that didn't matter because it didn't concern them and anyway it would be covered by the hem of her skirt, while if she wanted a quick moral boost at any time when in danger of doing something unsensible, particularly with Mr Stocks around, all she had to do was hitch the skirt up a little and take a quick peep at the message. It would, she thought, be very fortifying and seemed a logical and sensible thing to do.

Mr Rogers, however, thought she ought to be listening to him.

In the evening, Annabel went round to Kate's, partly so that they could do their French homework together but mainly to give her an opportunity to project sensible vibrations at Mr Stocks. It was a warm evening and he was sitting in a deckchair in the garden hidden behind a newspaper he was reading.

'Hallo, Mr Stocks,' Annabel called out brightly. 'Lovely evening.'

There was a grunt from behind the newspaper.

'Kate says you want to see how we handle the dinghy. That'll be lovely. Monday evening, you said.'

Another grunt, in a slightly lower tone.

Annabel and Kate sat down on a rustic bench, placing their books on a similarly rustic table, the top of which settled to one side slightly under the weight. The top rested on a stout central leg, a section of tree trunk with the bark still on it. The bench was composed of a rough-hewn plank resting on two shorter sections of tree trunk.

'I haven't seen all this before,' said Annabel. 'Is it new?'

'Dad's just made it,' whispered Kate, 'so don't criticize. Be careful, though. The bench is a bit unsteady.'

'I like them,' said Annabel. 'Your dad's very artistic, isn't he. He's always making something or painting pictures.'

Annabel, being artistic herself, appreciated creativity in others and was understanding about imperfections.

Before beginning the French, Kate noticed that Annabel produced a small card from her pocket which she propped up against a book where she could see it. On the card was printed: TRUST IN ALLAH BUT TIE UP YOUR CAMEL.

'It's an old Persian proverb,' said Annabel, seeing Kate's glance. 'I thought it might be useful to bear in mind.' They then discussed the homework, Annabel making a number of responsible-sounding remarks in case Mr Stocks happened to be listening.

He didn't appear to be doing so. He hadn't turned over a page for some time. When Kate went indoors for some drinks Annabel said to him, trying to establish friendly contact and find out if he were looking at the job adverts: 'Anything there, Mr Stocks?'

There was no reply at first from the invisible Mr Stocks and Annabel wondered if he were too wrapped up in his own unhappy thoughts to have heard. Suddenly, however, from behind the paper came a muttered growl.

'The whole thing makes you sick,' he said.

He folded up the newspaper, got up and went inside the house, passing Kate who was coming out with the drinks.

'Do you think Dad's noticed how sensible you've been?' she asked anxiously, sitting down again.

'I hope so,' said Annabel but she didn't sound very confident. 'I think he must have a lot on his mind though, like you were saying.'

Kate was only too glad to have an excuse for her father's behaviour.

When Annabel got home she found her own father in the sitting-room reading a book as he often was. This one was about eastern religions – she knew that because she had glanced through it earlier and it was from it that she had got the Persian proverb. Mr Bunce had a wide range of interests.

Annabel sat down opposite him. 'Good book, Dad?' she inquired after a while.

'Very,' replied Mr Bunce.

'I think you should have been a professor,' said Annabel. 'You'd have made a good professor.'

The remark seemed to please her father. He lowered the book.

'I'd have liked that,' he said. 'I often wish I could have gone on to university and become an academic.'

'Why didn't you?'

Mr Bunce looked wistful.

'It wasn't as easy as that. I had to leave school to get a job and earn some money.' He sighed. 'I was born just too soon, before so many young people started going to university. I didn't have the chances you young people have today. That's why you mustn't waste them . . .'

Annabel allowed him to continue on this familiar theme for a little while.

'I wonder if Kate's dad feels like that,' she murmured, almost to herself. 'Regretful.'

Mr Bunce caught the remark and considered it. He knew Kate's father, though not well, mainly through parents' evenings and other Willers functions. 'It's possible,' he said. 'What does he do? Works for some company on the industrial estate making things to do with electronics or something. Yes, he might well be someone who hasn't fulfilled himself.'

As far as Mr Bunce was concerned, anyone who had anything to do with electronics, however remote, must be unfulfilled. Like his daughter, he was a romantic and a dreamer. He turned to his book.

Annabel went up to her room and sat on her bed and thought about it.

'It must be terrible to be unfulfilled,' she thought, 'especially if you're artistic by nature. It's not surprising Mr Stocks gets a bit sour at times. I wish I could do something to help.'

She was sitting beneath a notice which she had pinned to the wall immediately after getting home from school. It read: ARE YOU THINKING CLEARLY?

'I think it's probably going to be all right,' said Kate at dinner break next day. 'Dad was in a better mood this morning. He said something about "when you two go

60

to Bungthorpe". Just a slip of the tongue, I suppose, but it sounds promising, doesn't it. I think you must have impressed him last night.'

They were sitting on their favourite bench again. Though still cautious Kate was today feeling more cheerful and optimistic. Watching Annabel trying to steer a course sensible enough to satisfy her father was nerve-racking but there was exhilaration, too, in watching sharp and slippery bends being safely negotiated.

'What were you talking to Deborah Breakspear about at break?' asked Kate.

This was the first chance she'd had to speak to Annabel properly today. Annabel had been late that morning and they hadn't met up with each other to walk to school as they usually did, and then at break she'd gone off with Deborah Breakspear and Kate had seen them walking up and down in earnest conversation. To tell the truth Kate had been just a little bit piqued because she'd had a distinct feeling of not being wanted, but that had been silly and she was over it now.

'Just this and that,' replied Annabel, vaguely. 'Her holidays, things like that.'

'Where's she going?'

'Portugal. Her parents have rented a villa on the Algarve for a month. They go off on the same day we go to Bungthorpe.'

Deborah's family was quite well off by Lord Willoughby's standards. Not in the same league as the Franks-Walters, of course, but they had a nice house with a paddock and orchard out on the Corton Compton road. Her father had his own business, something to do with printing and design. Deborah herself apart from being one of the nicest people in 3 G, was also one of the brainiest, invariably sharing top position in the class with Julian Parlane.

'Lucky Deborah!' said Kate.

'I'm quite happy going to Bungthorpe,' said Annabel.

'So am I, really,' said Kate. And she was.

As they rose to go indoors, Kate noticed that Annabel had a new message on the back of her hand. It said, simply: THINK.

That was on Wednesday. On Friday, amid the customary scenes of quiet jubilation and satisfaction, Lord Willoughby's broke up for the holidays.

2

By the following Monday evening when they were due to take the rubber dinghy down to the river to prove their competence, Kate was very happy and confident. Over the weekend she had bought, on impulse, a giant beach-ball which she had seen in a shop window at a bargain price. This dinghy business was, after all, just a formality to satisfy her father. She and Annabel were both good swimmers, very much at home in the water and very careful at the seaside; her father knew that.

He'd been in a bad mood when he suggested the trial, that was all. But he'd been in a better one the last few days. He and Annabel had been getting on rather well together.

Indeed, she'd noticed that Annabel had borrowed some of her father's water-colours – he had a heap of them in a cupboard – saying that she wanted to study them more closely. Clever old Annabel! She knew the way to her father's heart. Who said that Annabel wasn't sensible! She could win anybody over if she tried.

In this cheerful frame of mind Kate waited for her father to come home from work. He was late. The phone rang. It was Annabel wondering why Kate hadn't called for her yet.

'I'm waiting for Dad to get home. He's usually so prompt. He would have to be late tonight, wouldn't he, just when it's such a lovely evening and we're going out on the river. I'm really looking forward to playing with the dinghy now.'

So was Annabel. She was impatient to be off, as only Annabel could be impatient. It was a second-hand dinghy, bought cheaply with her own money, and she hadn't even tried it out yet. Couldn't the two of them at least take it down to the river now and blow it up and be all ready and waiting on the bank for when Mr Stocks arrived?

It was agreed with Kate's mother. Annabel and Kate would wait for him by the pool a little downstream from the bridge. Kate changed into shorts, T-shirt and plimsolls and lightheartedly set off to call for Annabel.

Mr Stocks, meanwhile, was late because he had been called to see Mr Hayraker, General Manager of the firm for which he worked, Beldews (Addendon) Ltd, a component part of the mighty Beldews (UK).

He was pleased to get the summons, assuming that the quality of his work had at last been noticed and was to be duly rewarded. The firm, after all, was doing well. But apparently not.

'I understand', said Mr Hayraker, when he had settled, 'that you are embittered.'

'What?' said Mr Stocks, startled. 'Who says?'

'Just about everybody in Addendon. It's a small place, especially if you're a member of the golf club, as I am. I hear that you're a frustrated artist, wasted in a place like Beldews and actively looking for a job more in keeping with your talents. Samples of your art, water-colours, I understand, have been sent to various prospective employers.'

'But –' said Mr Stocks.

'A young lady, a Miss Bunce, appears to be campaigning on your behalf. Actually, she rang me up for a chat this afternoon. She seemed to be trying to find out if there's a more suitable job for you within the firm.'

Mr Hayraker leaned back in his chair. He was a small, balding man in a blue pin-striped suit.

'What I can't understand,' he said, 'is why you're so special. Are your pictures any better than those?'

He waved his arm at the wall and Mr Stocks saw that a number of framed water-colours, of adequate though not outstanding quality, were hung there.

'Those are mine,' said Mr Hayraker. 'I'm a frustrated artist, too. I'm also a frustrated farmer. Every morning as I drive here in this glorious weather I look out of my car window and see the farmworkers out with their cattle and smell the hedgerows and listen to the birds singing and I crave to be there with them. With a name like mine I must have farming ancestors I suppose, and the urge is still there. Instead I have to come to this concrete and glass factory estate. Mind you, I also have an urge to be an airline pilot. The joy of being up there above the clouds! Come to think of it, I have an urge to be just about anything but sitting here.

'I don't suppose there's anybody in this building who isn't wishing they were doing something else but we all have to get on with it. I don't want people working here who can't control their discontent.'

*

As Annabel tremblingly pointed out when Mr Stocks eventually erupted by the river bank, she'd only been trying to help. It had seemed a good idea. He had, after all, sounded so fed up and said the whole thing made him sick and it's not very easy to sell yourself, especially if you're artistic, so she'd decided to have a go for him. She'd started by asking if Deborah Breakspear's father had any jobs available and it had sort of gone from there.

What had made him sick, Mr Stocks informed her, was simply the enormous salaries other people seemed to be getting for doing apparently very little. Yes, he had sat staring at the jobs page: comparing other people's rewards with his own and feeling envious. That was all. As for his artistic talents, he himself was long reconciled to the fact that, although he might have wished it otherwise, he didn't have any.

What he had *not* wanted was his career at Beldews, such as it was, ruined as it apparently had been. Thanks very much. Mr Hayraker had left him totally in the air about any action he might take but his manner had been caustic and threatening, to put it mildly.

Kate, listening anguished, thought he was over-reacting. Annabel may have been a little too en-thusiastic but she had only been doing her best for him. This, then, was why she had been cultivating Deborah Breakspear. For his sake! And such were her thanks! But what was going to happen to their holiday now?

Livid though he was, Mr Stocks did not allow what had happened to influence him as far as the dinghy trial was concerned. Having calmed himself with an effort he told them to get out on to the river.

As they launched the dinghy and scrambled in,

Kate found herself trembling from the strain of her father's outburst. Her first confused and splashing strokes with the paddle merely spun the dinghy on its axis and Annabel wasn't being any help. Glancing round, Kate saw why.

Annabel was in a worse state of nerves than she was herself. Her hands were shaking. And she wasn't paddling because she was engaged in what her presently over-strained mind evidently considered a more urgent task. She was trying to prop a card against the side of the dinghy where she'd be able to see it. The card stated in large, bold letters: THINK! THEN THINK AGAIN!

Not surprisingly, the card was refusing to stand up. As Kate watched, Annabel fumbled in her pocket and produced a large safety pin. Then, with one quick jab and a wiggle, she pushed the pin through card and rubber. It was done in a moment before Kate could get out her despairing warning screech. Annabel started, uttered a screech of her own, and pulled the pin out again.

The dinghy started to deflate quietly, without fuss.

There was really no need for the precipitate way in which Mr Stocks dashed into the water to help. The dinghy took some time to subside and the water was shallow and they were near the bank. He simply got himself as wet and muddy as they for no good reason. He was shouting all the time and when they were all out on the bank he was still shouting. What he was shouting, to Annabel, was:

'On no account will I allow you to go on holiday with my daughter. You would drown her. She will go alone and that is final.'

Annabel stood trembling before him. She was drenched and black mud clung to her legs almost to her knees. She was still holding the tethering cord of the deflated dinghy which she had hauled behind her out of the water. She was a sorry sight. But in Kate's eyes she had never had greater dignity.

'I'm sorry, Mr Stocks,' she said. 'I seem to have disappointed you generally today.'

Then she walked off along the bank without glancing at Kate, dragging the dinghy behind her. Kate, already despairing, had a sense of sudden, even stronger shock.

'Annabel!' she cried, sharply. 'Where are you going? We'll give you a lift home, won't we, Dad?'

Even Mr Stocks seemed disconcerted. 'Wait a minute,' he called. 'You can't walk home like that. You'll catch cold.'

Annabel only quickened her pace. Kate sprinted in pursuit. Her shorts flapped coldly wet against her and her plimsolls made sucking noises and oozed mud. 'Annabel! Don't be offended! Annabel!'

But Annabel wouldn't look round and Kate's father was calling her. He was angry again.

'Come home and get those wet clothes off, Kate. There's nothing you can do for Annabel if she won't let you.'

Annabel disappeared round a bend in the path, the dinghy slithering after her.

As Kate turned slowly round she saw a white card drifting along just below the surface of the river. The message on it, THINK! THEN THINK AGAIN!, was clearly visible. As she watched, it became water-logged and, turning slowly over, sank from view.

When Kate rang Annabel later that evening she was told she was up in her room.

'She said she wasn't to be disturbed by *anybody*,' said Mrs Bunce, unhappy and embarrassed at the emphasis. 'She was very firm about it, Kate. Has something been happening? She came back all wet and muddy. Is everything all right?'

'Everything's fine,' Kate lied, miserably.

'Can I give her a message?'

'Just – just to ring me as soon as she feels able to.'

Kate went into the sitting-room and sat down. Her father was in there determinedly reading a newspaper. Her mother was just sitting. There was an atmosphere. Kate went up to bed early.

Annabel didn't ring in the morning so Kate tried her again but she'd gone out. Mrs Bunce sounded even more embarrassed this time. The Bungthorpe holiday was beginning to seem almost of secondary importance now. Things had gone beyond that.

Unable to settle, Kate went out for a walk herself. It was a lovely summer's day, the sort of day that shouldn't be wasted but here she was wasting it. She wandered round the pond and past the church, looking at the roses and the honeysuckle and the plums and apples growing in the cottage gardens and thinking how mockingly beautiful things could be if there was no one to share them. She was deeply worried.

In the High Street, Miles Noggins was standing outside Strides the newsagents wolfing through a packet of crisps and he said hallo to her. A Martian monster dismounted from a motor-cycle pillion, removed its space helmet and became Justine Bird, with a brand new brilliant blonde hair-colour for the holidays. Her companion monster, the driver, followed suit revealing a coxcomb of flaming red hair; a new 'feller', a holiday 'feller' perhaps. They disappeared into one of the shops together, perhaps in search of more hair dye or some holiday fags.

Lord Willoughby's was on holiday, its released prisoners all out enjoying themselves each in their own way.

All of them, that is, except Kate. Her pace slowed still further. Where could she go? What could she do? Outside the Post Office she paused, looking irresolutely at the phone box. Should she try Annabel again?

And then out of the Post Office, walking firmly and purposefully, came Annabel.

At the sight of her, Kate's heart lifted.

'Annabel!' she cried. 'Annabel. There you are!'

Annabel saw her and hesitated. She seemed disconcerted. For a moment it appeared that she might be about to say something then her face clouded and her nose lifted slightly and she walked on.

'Annabel!' cried Kate again, anguished. She trotted in pursuit. 'Annabel, even if we can't go on holiday together, we –'

It wasn't having any effect. Annabel was ignoring her.

'Oh, Annabel!' she cried yet again, this time in despair. But Annabel simply walked on.

The unbelievable had happened. Annabel had snubbed her.

3

'It's only temporary,' Kate told herself that evening. 'Of course Annabel's offended. Who wouldn't be after being treated like that. But she'll come round.'

There was an atmosphere at home again. Kate's father was going around with a woodenly stubborn expression on his face which proclaimed, 'I will *not* change my mind.'

That night, before going to sleep, Kate decided that

she would go and call on Annabel next day. She would confront her.

She set off at half past nine the following morning. It was another mockingly cloudless day. But though she had been restless till setting off she found herself walking progressively more slowly. It was nervousness. The very idea! Nervous of meeting Annabel!

She had just turned the corner into Badger's Close when a car followed and overtook her, slowing as it did so. It stopped outside a house not far in front of her. Surely – yes! – outside number 9, Annabel's house! The driver hooted twice and the nearside rear door swung open. The car was picking someone up.

Kate halted. She was now able to catch a glimpse of the profile of the rear seat passenger who had opened the door.

It was Deborah Breakspear.

The driver, a man, was just visible beyond her. Presumably it was her father. They must be waiting for Annabel. Annabel was going somewhere with Deborah. A feeling of exclusion crawled, icy-fingered, over Kate.

Had Annabel found a new friend? Had she, Kate, been dropped?

Deborah was, after all, so nice. Not only brainy and athletic and good at everything and well-off, but nice.

Wretchedness clutched at Kate. What had she got to offer anyway except a miserable, bad-tempered, ungrateful father?

It was lucky she hadn't been noticed by Deborah. She mustn't be seen now, not at this of all times, obviously on her way to call for Annabel when Annabel was going somewhere with someone else to which she wasn't invited. How pathetic that would look!

Close behind her was the cypress hedge bordering the garden of number 3. It was still young and not too dense and Kate stepped into it, making sure the branches hid her on both sides, cringing into as small a space as possible. How appropriately abject it felt to have to cringe like that! She felt like being abject, the more abject the better. She hoped no one would look out of the window of number 3 and see her but she didn't really care.

If she peered through one side of the hedge she could see the Breakspears' car; through the other, the Bunces' front door beyond an array of HT roses and flowering cherry saplings. How well she knew that front door! How many times she had passed through it, with Annabel, laughing and happy. And now . . . now she was excluded, an alien, a spy. Abject wasn't a strong enough word. There wasn't a strong enough word in the English language.

No sign of Annabel yet. There was another hoot, then the car door opened and slammed. Mr Breakspear came into Kate's field of vision, sauntering down the path to the Bunces' front door followed by Deborah.

Suddenly the front door opened and Annabel emerged. No, not emerged; erupted, smiling and waving with her right hand; she was carrying a rolled up towel under her left arm. She was, Kate realized with another chill, choking feeling, going swimming with Deborah. Mr Breakspear must have taken time off from his business to drive them to the big outdoor pool at Querminster.

Then Annabel wasn't sitting at home, as Kate in her folly had imagined she might be, moping at not being allowed to go to Bungthorpe, miserable at the rift with her best friend. No, she was off, laughing and carefree, to have fun with her new friend.

Hallo! There was a minor contretemps. Annabel, with all her laughing and waving on the doorstep, had allowed the door to close on the corner of her rolled up towel and as she moved forward the towel was pulled from under her arm and her bathing suit fell out.

There was more laughing and now Deborah was picking up the bathing suit and Annabel was opening and closing the door again to get the towel out and Mr Breakspear was looking on chuckling indulgently and apparently enjoying himself. What a jolly-looking, tweedy sort of person he was!

How different, Kate thought miserably; how kindly and tolerant Mr Breakspear seemed when compared with her own embittered and snarling father! There was Annabel behaving as unsensibly as she ever did and was Mr Breakspear complaining? No, not he! He was enjoying the fun. Annabel was good enough for the Breakspears. Why wasn't she good enough for the Stocks?

Yes. Annabel was right. She always was. Other people didn't always realize it but Kate knew that beneath that apparently unsensible exterior lay a brilliant and perceptive mind, and Annabel had shown her perception yet again. Though he might try to disguise it, Mr Stocks *was* embittered. It was awful for him, certainly, but did his family have to keep on paying for it *always*?

Annabel was walking towards the Breakspears' car, chattering cheerfully at the top of her voice. Kate didn't want to listen but if it were forced upon her then . . . what was Annabel saying? Something about 'holiday'? Yes – 'it's only four days now till we go on holiday,' she had said.

What holiday? She had been banned from going on holiday with Kate so – so did she mean she was going to Portugal with the Breakspears?

Despite the warmth, Kate turned to ice. She heard the car doors slam again and the engine start up and she had the presence of mind to squeeze through the hedge and crouch in the garden of number 3 for a few moments while it turned in the road and drove away in the direction from which it had come.

So Annabel was going to Portugal with Deborah Breakspear!

She was weeping as she walked home, allowing her face to crumple and the tears to course down without check. There was no one about to see it. The estate was deserted in the heat. Probably everyone else had gone off to swim or walk or was already away on holiday. The whole population of Addendon was enjoying itself. Only she, Kate, was here alone, friendless, aimless, walking the pavements that were hot beneath the thin soles of her sandals.

Then Annabel would be in Portugal for a month. Leaving her to go to Bungthorpe alone for a week.

Bungthorpe! How pathetic the very name seemed now, though probably it always had been. How pathetic the idea of spending a week in her grandparents' bungalow when compared with a villa on the Algarve!

After a month on the Algarve together Annabel and Deborah would no doubt return as inseparables, intimates, their friendship consolidated and honed by happy memories of togetherness with sea and sand and sun and sailing and flamenco dancing and all the other things that people do on the Algarve, whatever they might be. Kate herself wouldn't know. She'd never been there. Wasn't likely to as far as she could see. Never even been abroad. Not to Majorca or anywhere. Oh yes, she had, come to think of it. She'd been on a day trip to Boulogne.

And then, next term, Annabel would change her seat in class. She wouldn't want to sit next to Kate any longer. She'd sit next to Deborah, her new friend. She, Kate, would have to watch them out of the corner of her eye, whispering together and remembering all the good times they'd had in Portugal. She herself would have to find another friend. But she didn't want another friend. She only wanted Annabel.

Thus tormented, Kate wandered the streets of Addendon. She didn't want to go home and sit alone in her hot room or in the claustrophobic garden. Instead she trailed along the High Street once more looking in the shop windows, returning home only for lunch before going out again to sit by the pond and watch the ducks.

At supper her mother was abstracted while her father glared at the newspaper in a defiant sort of way. Her brother Robert, who lived in something of a world of his own, was clearly puzzled.

'Quiet, isn't it,' he said, when the sound of clashing cutlery, scraping chair-legs and turning newspaper pages seemed particularly loud.

No one took any notice.

'Maybe it just seems quiet', he continued, 'because your friend Annabel hasn't been round for at least half an hour. Haven't split up, have you?'

Tears started to Kate's eyes.

'It's strange, isn't it,' said her mother, in an abstracted sort of way, 'how friendships come and go when you're young. People can be so close one minute and the next they can't think what they saw in each other.'

Mrs Stocks appeared to be speaking generally, not alluding to any specific case.

'People grow apart,' she continued, philosophically, 'especially when they're young. The clever ones sort themselves out and go off with each other so there's often a lot of changing friendships at school. Especially, I always think, around the third year at secondary school.'

It dawned upon Kate that this was supposed to be comforting. Her biased mother was hinting that she, Kate, her daughter, was the clever one who would find someone of her own mental stature to chum up with now that the lunatic Annabel was out of the way. As comfort it was worse than unsuccessful. She got up.

'Thanks for supper, Mum,' she said in a high-pitched voice. She left the table and went up to her room and sat on her bed.

Presumably her mother would not have tried such condolence if she had known that Annabel was now friends with the brainiest girl in 3G, who always vied with Julian Parlane to be top of the class. If the clever ones were sorting themselves out then it was she, Kate, who was being left out in the cold.

As she reflected upon that, a feeling of comparative tranquillity descended upon Kate. Perhaps, after all, her mother's words did bring a certain sort of comfort. Not relief or happiness, certainly not that, but – but perhaps an *acceptance*.

'It may be', thought Kate, 'that this would have happened sooner or later anyway and that it's just as well that it's sooner. I couldn't hold Annabel back. She's got to move on to more interesting people than me. I only come about fourth or fifth in the class – come to think of it, that's higher than Annabel usually, but that's because she's got so many things on her mind . . . yes, for Annabel's sake I'm glad it's happened. It's a sacrifice but perhaps it won't be in vain.'

While sitting there in this noble mood of self-sacrifice and self-abasement Kate heard the phone ring downstairs and dashed down to answer it in the wild hope that it might be Annabel.

But it wasn't. It was for Robert and she ascended the stairs to her room again, slowly, her mood of nobility returning, to spend the evening in dignified, if not exactly happy, repose.

4

And the next day dawned bleakly as the general feeling of catastrophe on waking translated itself into the particular remembrance that Annabel had a new best friend.

In the morning Kate did some housework for her mother, cleaning the bath and basins and dusting but as she contemplated the empty afternoon ahead she knew there was only one thing she wanted to do with it. She wanted to spend it remembering Annabel and all the good times they had had together; to revisit old haunts; yes, to make a sort of pilgrimage.

There would be comfort in that; and beauty. Immediately after lunch, she set off.

But where to start? Every street, every corner was haunted by the spirit of Annabel, her lost friend. By the corner of Woodland Grove she paused. Already she was at key point in her journey.

It was somewhere along there, on a bitterly cold, blustery March day seven years ago that they had first met. Kate had just arrived in Addendon for the very first time in the back of her parents' car. She had known somewhere in the back of her mind that they were going to look at houses and that they might be going to live there and she had had mixed feelings about that. There was a big boy at her previous school who used to chase her and try to punch her so she'd be glad to get away from him; on the other hand she loved the teddy-bears on her bedroom wallpaper and didn't want to leave them. So she had had an open mind as they drove towards Addendon.

Their arrival put a stop to that. It had started to snow as they got out of the nice warm car and Kate had jumped out into a pool of mud. The estate was only just being built and as a place to live in it had looked horrifying; a desolation of heaps of mud chewed up by bulldozer tracks; stacks of pipes and bricks and cables; heaps of rubble from previous demolition work; uprooted trees.

Some of the fallen branchwood was being burnt on a huge bonfire which someone had been silly enough to light despite the wind and a pall of smoke trailed over the whole scene. Woodland Grove, like Badger's Close and Oakwood Crescent, was nothing more than a bumpy, new-laid track curving through the mud.

Over this purgatorial wasteland roared the wind, carrying the thickening snow before it.

Kate had howled and refused to hold her mother's hand. Her father had disappeared and returned with a thickset man in a duffle coat who kept guffawing about nothing and slapping her father on the back and giving him bits of paper with brightly coloured pictures of houses on them.

Teeth bared against the wind, they had fought their way through the mud to stand and look at something. What? Apparently the place they were to live in. But it hadn't been a house at all, just the pattern of a house on the ground, in fact not even that. Some of it was just a hole in the ground.

Kate didn't want to live in a hole in the ground in this horrible place. She stood and howled louder. Other people and their howling children were moving about in the snow. A small, howling fat boy was being propelled along by the force of smacks from behind, doled out by a stout father. 'I'll give it to you when you get home, Miles Noggins,' the stout father was snarling. Lord Willoughby's of the future was assembling itself.

Then out of the snow wandered an apparition; a girl of Kate's own age dressed in a brilliant red anorak, its hood fringed with white fur out of which peeped a pink face, and equally brilliant red boots with white tops. This apparition, like a miniature Santa Claus, had instantly transformed the scene in Kate's eyes, making it Christmassy and jolly, and she had quietened down.

'What's your name?' the apparition had said.

'Kate.'

'Mine's Annabel.' The apparition had continued to loiter, studying her intently.

'Where is this place?' Kate had asked, still inclined to be tearful. 'I know it starts with "A".'

'Alaska,' the Annabel girl had replied.

(This was, of course, incorrect but Kate was very ready to accept it since she had recently seen something on television about Alaska. The film had shown scenes of driving snow and men crouched against the wind constructing something, scenes very similar to those now in front of her. What Kate didn't realize was that Annabel had seen the same film and was jumping to conclusions.)

Kate didn't want to live in Alaska. The film had gone on to talk about dark and frozen winters and being cut off by ice and something about polar bears. She had started to howl again.

'I've got a secret den,' Annabel had said, casually. Taking Kate by the hand she had led her away and Kate, silenced by this wondrous revelation, had acquiesced willingly. They pointed their anorak hoods into the wind and plodded away, hands tightly clasped, while somewhere nearby the thickset man was continuing to clap Mr Stocks on the back and bellow into his ear further information about the difference between the Regency-style semi and the Jacobean.

'It's a *warm* secret den,' Annabel had said.

They had been discovered some half an hour later playing nurses and patients in a bedroom in the show house. It took longer to discover than it should have done because Annabel, in order to turn it into a truly *secret* den, had removed the keys from the door where they had been left and placed them on a ledge in the hall after first locking the door. This meant that the guffawing man, no longer guffawing, found himself confronted by a locked door and a queue of shivering and irritable people waiting to look around the show house and had to go off on a long search for his assistant who held the only spare keys. The assistant was himself already searching for two small girls reported missing by their frantic parents, named Stocks and Bunce respectively, who were convinced they must be wedged in a drain pipe or have been run over by a bulldozer.

By the time they were discovered Annabel and Kate had played, besides nurses and patients, cooks in the kitchen and waitresses and customers in the dining-room. The sign outside the show house had, after all, urged them to come inside, look around and make themselves at home.

Kate's parents, instead of showing their relief with shouts and smacks as they did, might actually have been grateful if they'd known that Kate and Annabel had sworn a pact of lifelong friendship and that Kate was now not only reconciled to living in Alaska but desperate to do so as quickly as possible because she associated it with Annabel. Or perhaps they mightn't.

They'd moved there four months later, not to Woodland Grove but to Oakwood Crescent, and Kate had immediately gone off in search of Annabel and found her swinging on a gate in Badger's Close. A tear rolled out of Kate's eyes now as she recalled the reunion.

She walked on through Addendon, past the Junior School at the bottom of Gamble Street, its yelling playground stilled now for the holidays, where she and Annabel had once spent an afternoon trapped on the roof.

And the Church Hall: memories of Brownies and sitting on the fence outside with Annabel waiting for Brown Owl to arrive on her bike with the key: the discovery that Brown Owl was Damian Price's mother in disguise and that the reason she was in-variably late for Brownies was not because she had been out flitting round the hedgerows finding mice for her owlets' supper, as Annabel had always main-tained but, more prosaically, was giving Damian and his five older brothers their tea.

Annabel had been the only First Addendon Brownie to fail her Hostess Badge first time and it had all been on behalf of Kate. She had been entertaining her guest with tea, sandwiches and light hostessy conversation when it had emerged that the guest was none other than Mrs Cork from the Post Office whose daughter Clemmie was a sixer who had been pushing Kate around and being beastly to her. Annabel had instantly removed the cup from Mrs Cork's hand and taken away the sandwiches and refused to hand them over, subsequently eating them herself in a corner rather than waste them. Kate wept as she remembered that now. There had never been a more loyal friend than Annabel.

Strides, the newsagents in the High Street; it still had metal advertisements for long-forgotten brands of cigarettes outside its dark brown door. Kate went in there and bought some chocolate now for old time's sake.

She and Annabel had always preferred it to the newer, smarter newsagents at the other end of the High Street because Mr Stride was so nice and didn't mind them hanging around reading the comics and looking at the fashion magazines and was willing to give Annabel tick.

He had his limits though as Kate discovered now, when he asked her where her friend was and would she remind her that sixty pence had been outstanding for over two months. Kate fumbled in her pocket and continued her pilgrimage sixty pence the poorer.

The Memorial Hall: many a function they had attended there; many a time they had been asked to leave it. Kate went inside. The main hall was filled with chairs ready for the next production by the Addendon Players and she sat down on one, third row from the back, four seats along. It was the very seat she had been asked to leave when she and Annabel, who had been sitting on her right, had been ejected from the last production.

The play had seemed quite safe, no deep tragedy for Annabel to become upset and weep noisily over, not so hilarious that she would slowly subside howling under the chairs of the people in front, upsetting them. No emotional music, which was much the riskiest of all. Kate had settled down to enjoy it. Alas! Annabel's sympathies had gone out to young Ewan McLure, the only non-adult in the cast who was in the Second Year at Lord Willoughby's. He had had quite a large part in which he was obviously out of his depth and Annabel had sought to bolster him by laughing and applauding at his every entrance and utterance till it had got on people's nerves.

Kate sat there with her memories for a few moments then rose to leave. In the entrance hall she paused to let two youths go in front of her. Sleek from the showers, they were emerging from the gym which had been built as an extension to the hall and was much used for keeping fit and such things as yoga classes. They must have been having their workouts. One was well-built and muscular, the other spindly and apparently muscle-less.

'I can tell it's working,' the spindly one was saying. 'I got to the pain barrier today.'

His evident pride was given short shrift by the muscular one. 'That's no good,' he replied, scornfully.

'No?'

'Nar,' the other's voice had all the authority of his muscles. 'You gotta *get* to the pain barrier, then you gotta go *through* it till you find yourself gettin' sorta *numb*. *Then* you know you're gettin' somewhere.'

'Oh!'

They passed out of the door and Kate slowly followed. She knew how the spindly one felt. She was at the pain barrier over Annabel. Perhaps in time she'd go through it and become numb and start getting somewhere but it wasn't happening yet.

In the early evening she wandered along the path by the river where the woods came down to it. This was all Annabel country, every pool and tree and flower and spotted red toadstool of it. Deep in the woods the path came to an end at an old, broken wall, so moss-covered that the stone was almost invisible, and there she halted.

It was on the other side of this wall that they had had their own private dell, their permanent secret den. They had found it in early spring, a knobbly green hollow where a tiny tributary entered the river, covered in snowdrops and crocuses and made private by bushes. There was an old disused boathouse there and it had become all their own. They had come there through the spring and the summer and seen the daffodils and bluebells come out, and the bushes had blossomed with wondrously sweet-smelling and cultivated-looking flowers. They had put bits of carpet and curtains in the boathouse and pinned pictures cut from magazines to the wall. Outside, they had made a little garden and transplanted bulbs and planted seeds.

It wasn't till late summer that they discovered their little paradise was in someone's garden. The house lay on the other side of the bushes. A man came and chased them away.

Come to think of it, thought Kate, to be with Annabel had always been to be chased away and thrown out of so many places, to be shouted at by so many people.

She walked back along the river bank. The sun had sunk behind the trees and the warmth had given way to a little nostalgic breeze that idled amongst the leaves. The moon was out though the sky was still light.

'But', Kate said to the moon, 'Annabel was my friend and I wouldn't have changed her for anything.'

The next day was Friday, the last before Annabel would depart for Portugal and she for Bungthorpe. *If* she were going to Bungthorpe! She didn't want to. The thought of sitting alone on that train was unbearable.

It was during the afternoon that Kate decided she had come through the pain barrier and was at the numb stage. She came to a decision.

From the cupboard she took the giant beach-ball she had bought for Bungthorpe. She was going to present it to Annabel, not personally – she wasn't going to be accused, even by herself, of inventing a reason to see Annabel – no, she would leave it with a note on her doorstep. It would be a gesture to show Annabel that she understood.

She got paper and pen and wrote:

Dear Annabel,
I hope you have a lovely time in Portugal. I'd like you to have this beach-ball as a going away present and I hope you and Deborah will play with it and have lots of fun. As you know, I shall be at Bungthorpe but I shall think of you and hope you are having as good a time as I shall be.

Yours,
Kate

She avoided letting a tear fall on to it because that wouldn't have been fair. As it was, it seemed very dignified. After reflecting, she changed the *Kate* to *Kate Stocks*.

Then she left the house with the ball and the note in a large paper bag.

But she'd been fooling herself. She wasn't through

the pain barrier at all. She was right in the middle of it. Tears were coursing uncontrollably down her cheeks as she went down the garden path, the beach-ball cradled in her arms in front of her. She tried to open the garden gate but her vision was too blurred. She couldn't find the latch. She tried to fumble for it and then gave up even that and just stood there shaking. Then, before she could adjust her mind to what was happening, there was a patter of running footsteps and the gate was flung violently open from the other side.

'Oh, Kate, I'm sorry,' wailed a well-known voice. 'I wasn't looking where I was going.'

Simultaneous with that the beach-ball burst, punctured by the prong of the latch which had caught it centrally. It had proved a flimsy product. It wouldn't have been worth the trouble of transporting to Portugal anyway.

'Are you all right, Kate? Have I hurt you? Kate, what's the matter? You're crying.'

'I'm all right,' said Kate automatically. Was this an hallucination? Was this what happened after the numbness?

Annabel came into focus as she wiped her eyes. She was now capering around triumphantly, waving something in her right hand.

'Cheer up, Kate. Look, I've got it.'

The situation was not easy to adapt to. 'Got what?' inquired Kate tremulously. It was difficult to feel anything and perhaps she didn't really want to for it might be tempting fate, because surely what was happening now must prove to be an illusion produced out of her fevered mind, and in a moment it would have melted away again and she would be plodding along Oakwood Crescent with the stupid beach-ball in her arms.

'My Life-Saving Certificate. I've been working for it all week. Got it in the nick of time. When your dad sees this he'll let me go to Bungthorpe with you.'

'Bungthorpe,' said Kate. 'But – aren't you going to Portugal with Deborah Breakspear – ?'

'Sorry about cutting you in the street.' Annabel was still waltzing around confusingly. 'But I knew you'd understand when I explained. I made a solemn vow I wasn't going to speak to you again till I'd got this certificate – what did you say about Portugal? Deborah Breakspear? What *are* you talking about, Kate? Deborah was doing a life-saving course as well and her father was running her to the swimming pool so I cadged a lift every day.'

'Can – can I see that certificate?' asked Kate. She was allowing her mind to accept, cautiously, that this might be reality after all. The beach-ball and note fell, forgotten, to the ground.

'I don't see how your dad can possibly refuse to let me go with you now,' cried Annabel as she passed it over. 'That'll show you're safe in my hands, won't it, Kate.'

'It wasn't the certificate itself,' said Mr Stocks approvingly that evening. Even more impressive and important was the determined and sensible way Annabel had gone about getting it. They were in the Stocks' dining-room and everyone was all smiles.

Yes, this was exactly the sort of evidence of good sense he had needed to see and certainly as far as he was concerned Annabel and Kate could go to Bungthorpe together with his blessing. Mrs Stocks smiled and nodded her agreement.

Having delivered this dignified and Olympian judgement Mr Stocks fled to the garden, there to raise his eyes jubilantly to high heaven and shake his own hands above his head. This was in sheer blessed relief that, as might have been said in other quarters, a face-saving formula had been found for ending the dispute which was all he now cared about. He had been looking forward in deep and desperate dread, as had Mrs Stocks, to Saturday morning and Kate having to be put on the train for Bungthorpe in floods of tears.

As he had said despairingly and privately to his wife, they might just as well go off and be drowned as that. The situation had become intolerable and he was enveloped now by a warm glow of regard and gratitude for Annabel. The dear girl had saved the situation.

There was another reason for his gratitude, though not one that he was going to let her know about. That afternoon he had been called to see Mr Hayraker. He had gone with a sick feeling that this might be the end of his career with Beldews. Instead, he had been told he was getting a rise and treated with a certain new respect and deference.

'I suppose I might have been taking you a little for granted,' Mr Hayraker had acknowledged. 'But you have only yourself to blame, you know. If you're unhappy you ought to say so instead of going round looking for other jobs. I hope you'll settle down now. If anything ever bothers you at all just let me know, and do remember the firm has an Arts Club.'

Mr Stocks had assured him he would and Mr Hayraker had courteously got up and held the door open for him to leave.

No, he certainly wasn't going to tell Annabel about that. It was the sort of thing which could undermine a young person's attitude to what was or was not good sense. However ... in a mood of warm benignity verging on euphoria Mr Stocks went indoors and found his wallet.

'While I think about it,' he said to Annabel and Kate who were sitting on the sofa making up for several days lost conversation, 'I'd like to give you both a little present to go to Bungthorpe with.' Before their grateful and widening eyes he started taking out notes. When was he going to stop?

At 8.25 on the following morning Kate's father pulled up outside Annabel's home in Badger's Close and hooted twice. Kate hung her head out of the rear window eagerly. Mr Stocks had offered to run them to the main line station at Querminster. Ahead lay two new firsts – the first time on holiday without parents and first time changing trains alone. Kate had a page of written instructions from her mother.

The only immediate response to the hoots was the opening of the next door neighbour's window and a glare from Mrs Piper herself. Not seeing this, Mr Stocks hooted twice more.

The Bunces' front door opened and there emerged, not Annabel, but Mrs Bunce. She dashed to the gate.

'She'll be with you in a moment, Mr Stocks,' she cried. 'Just getting her suitcase closed.' She dashed back indoors and the front door swung to again.

'I think I can see where Annabel gets it from,' chuckled Mr Stocks. How very genial he was this morning! Genial, with a hint of nervousness, too.

The front door opened again and this time it was Annabel. She was waving excitedly and she, too, dashed to the gate.

''Lo, Mr Stocks, 'lo, Kate. Be with you in a minute,' she called. Then she too dashed back again and once more the front door slid to.

'It'll be her father next time,' chuckled Mr Stocks, switching off the engine. He glanced at his watch and his expression became more thoughtful.

Next time it was Annabel and her mother, Annabel in the lead carrying a suitcase, one fastener of which was undone, while her mother carried two bags. Mr Stocks got out of the car and opened the boot and assisted them to put the luggage inside and then Annabel scrambled in beside Kate and she was saying goodbye to her mother through the open window and Mrs Bunce was calling about whether she'd got the list of instructions safely and Annabel was saying that she had and Mr Stocks was starting the engine and looking at his watch again and driving away and then at the end of the road he suddenly realized that the waves that Mrs Bunce had been directing after the car had become frantic beckonings instead and he was stopping, doing a three point turn in the road and Annabel was opening the window again to hear her mother shouting 'Your money . . . you've forgotten your money, Annabel . . .'

And Annabel was snatching her purse through the car window and Mr Stocks was doing a three point turn again, no longer looking genial but quite panic-stricken really . . .

They were off to Bungthorpe.

Annabel and the rabbit

*****

1

When Kate's father drove home after seeing her and Annabel off on the train to Bungthorpe he found himself compulsively contemplating the range of disasters which might befall them. The possibilities – assuming they succeeded in getting to Bungthorpe – seemed to be something like:

drowning; falling off a cliff – but, come to think of it, there weren't any cliffs at Bungthorpe, in which case . . . falling off the sea wall; being caught far out on the sand by the incoming tide and overwhelmed; stung by dangerous jellyfish; run over; falling out of the Big Wheel (he was running out of ideas); thrown by a runaway beach donkey . . .

No. He was groping. Odd, once you started to think about it, how narrow was the range of potential disasters. How did people come to have so many? But that certainly seemed to be a fairly comprehensive list . . . what others could there be?

Which just goes to show how unimaginative Kate's father was.

Annabel and Kate arrived at Bungthorpe in the late afternoon, when the day's heat was fading and the town was full of bronzed and peeling people drifting from the beach. They were met at the station by Kate's grandparents.

Bungthorpe is the focal point of what the writer of its holiday guide, though no one else, has called 'the East Coast côte d'Azur'. It is a very popular holiday resort attracting numerous visitors in summer.

In appearance, it is not unlike an American cow-town of the Wild West era. Its main street, Marine Prospect, is lined with gaudily painted swing half-doors, similar to the entrances to saloons, which give on to cavernous amusement arcades, interspersed with fish and chip cafés and places selling Bung-thorpe rock, beach necessities, souvenirs and so on. The whole ensemble throbs and thumps with pop music.

Marine Prospect makes straight as an arrow for the sea but despite its name the beach can no longer be seen from it, having disappeared when the new sea wall was built after the East Coast floods, shutting off the end of the street abruptly.

The sea can usually be heard growling and swishing about somewhere in the background but it chiefly makes its presence felt by the wind which comes off it, gritty with sand, and funnels along Marine Prospect sending old fish and chip papers and potato crisp bags swirling along the pavements to pile up in corners.

Leather-clad youths stride arrogantly out of the amusement arcades, kicking the doors aside as if they have just satisfactorily completed a shoot-out with the sheriff, and ride off on large shiny black motor-cycles, scattering holidaymakers. Their places are taken by other motorcyclists, fresh contingents of which constantly roar in to keep the holidaymakers on their toes.

To the north, the town merges into vast chalet and

caravan sites in which people have been known to wander about for hours looking for a way out. To the south, after an interval of open space largely occupied by rubbish dumps, a sewage works, a gasometer and a small 'holiday camp', there begins a huge area of dunes partly used by the RAF as a bombing range and by the army for exercises.

Annabel thought it was marvellous.

She had been telling Kate that she could smell the sea while the train was still ten miles distant, and certainly the combination of rotting seaweed and fish and chips was now deliciously strong. Kate savoured it too as they drove along Marine Prospect in her grandparents' car.

'You're so lucky to live here,' sighed Annabel. 'I can't wait to retire and come and live in a place like this, can you, Kate?'

'We don't live in Bungthorpe itself,' Kate's grandad explained as he drove. 'We're in Norby-on-Sea which is a kind of suburb beyond the caravan parks. It's about five minutes' drive. Bungthorpe's full name is really Bungthorpe-cum-Norby.'

He was a relaxed and amiable man, smoking a short pipe, who had come to Bungthorpe for the sea fishing and bowls. His wife, now growing stout, was constantly smiling, double chins quivering a little as she knitted. They were nice grandparents to have, they had always spoiled Kate when they could, and she appreciated them.

It was soon clear, however, that they felt their responsibilities. Perhaps something had been said to them by Kate's parents.

'What sort of things are you thinking of doing, dear?' Kate's gran asked, a little cautiously, speaking to either one of them, as they drove past the caravan sites.

'Oh, everything,' said Kate. 'When it's nice we'll go on the beach and swim and we're going to hire surf boards.'

'And when it's not,' said Annabel, 'we can go on the big dipper and all the other things, and then we want to explore.'

'We thought we might hire some bikes,' said Kate, 'and go along the coast.'

'There are all those dunes and marshes and enormous beaches and nature reserves.'

'We can lend you a couple of bikes,' said Grandad. 'Just one thing, though. If you go southwards watch out for warning notices and whatever you do don't go beyond them when the red flag's flying. There's an RAF range not far from here. They drop bombs twice à week. And sometimes the army joins in as well.'

'Oh, we wouldn't do anything as silly as that, would we, Kate?' said Annabel, laughing.

Kate was laughing, too. 'We may be silly at times, Grandad, but that's going a bit far.'

'As if we'd get bombed,' chuckled Annabel.

Norby-on-Sea, though so near, is a very different place from metropolitan Bungthorpe. At Norby live the people who run Bungthorpe, the owners of its caravan sites, its amusement arcades and other pleasures. Some of the residents of Norby, although they look quite ordinary and speak with quite ordinary accents, are millionaires. You would think that in this position they would want to spend all their time having goes on their own big dippers and playing with their own electronic games and all the other things, but oddly enough they seldom go to Bungthorpe themselves and grumble if, for business reasons, they have to.

Even more oddly, they refuse to allow any of these

pleasures to be constructed near their own homes and are up in arms immediately if there's so much as a suggestion of putting even one slot machine anywhere in Norby.

Norby is quiet, therefore, with a sandy beach backed by beach huts, a pretty High Street, many large Victorian houses and numerous old cottages, in one of which Kate's grandparents now lived.

None of which mattered to Annabel and Kate. All that concerned them was that the cottage, though tiny, was lovely with a quaintly irregular little spare room, whitewashed, with a sloping ceiling, into which the sun streamed in the mornings; that the garden was crowded with roses and honeysuckle and that it was only two minutes walk from the sea.

Sufficient it were to be in Bungthorpe-cum-Norby. For Bungthorpe-cum-Norby were paradise enow.

On Tuesday they went for their long bike ride. It was a lovely day, not too hot, they were tanned from two days of surfing and feeling athletic and adventurous.

The roads were ironing-board flat with little traffic on them and ran for the most part beside willow-lined dykes. Curves were kept for special occasions. These roads liked to run ruler-straight ahead and when they did turn, to do so sharply, preferably at a 90-degree angle. A subtly evocative vegetable smell, as of ripe cabbages, hung in the air.

They rode inland for a mile or two then turned left to go southwards parallel with the coast behind Bungthorpe and its chains of caravan and chalet parks which gave way to rubbish dumps and sewage works and gasometer before all that, too, came to an end and there was just the sea wall and a feeling of spaciousness and loneliness and the humming of tyres.

'Bliss!' said Annabel, contentedly.

At a sharp right-hand bend a narrower road went off to the left, heading straight for the dunes and the sea which lay beyond. It had a cul-de-sac sign at the entrance and led, apparently, only to a few farms. It looked so inviting that, at Annabel's suggestion, they set off to explore it.

They were glad they did. This little road did have curves in it, twisting between great boles of trees that crowded right to the edge of it, before straightening out again between high hedges full of dog roses.

Some cawing rooks emphasized the atmosphere of silent solitude and summer peace broken only by the two boys who appeared cycling fast towards them, taking advantage of the gentle slope down from the dunes to get up speed. The leading one sat up straight, one hand on the handlebars with the other held out to balance, knees akimbo as his legs flailed round, the other crouched low, pedalling furiously.

They were drawing near Annabel, who was ahead of Kate, when a rabbit ran out from the hedge on Annabel's side of the road. Seeing the cyclists converging upon it, it hesitated, panicked, seemed about to run in various directions and then dashed straight in front of the boys' bicycles. It realized its mistake as the first boy swerved and managed to avoid it, and it turned back, only to dodge in front of the second boy who had jammed on his brakes and was now swinging his front wheel to one side and putting his left foot down in an emergency stop. The wheel caught the rabbit a glancing blow.

Such was its own momentum that the rabbit, knocked sideways, rolled over several times, recrossing Annabel's path, before picking itself up and making off through the hedge from which it had first appeared. But there was something wrong. It was staggering.

'It's hurt,' shrieked Annabel who, pedalling slowly, had been able to halt her bicycle almost the instant the rabbit had appeared. 'Kate, it's broken its leg.'

Putting her bicycle against the hedge she ran to a gate and peered into the field, wringing her hands. 'Poor little thing,' she wailed. 'Look at it, Kate – look at the way it's running. It's in pain. Let's go after it.'

'Don't be daft,' one of the boys was shouting. 'You'll never catch it.' But Annabel was already scrambling over the gate and Kate, loyal as ever, propped her bike against Annabel's and set off in her wake. She could see the rabbit, still panic-stricken, bobbing and lurching across the fields towards the dunes. Hampered by its injured leg, it looked catchable.

But, wondered Kate as she panted in pursuit of Annabel, what would they do if they caught it? How could they help?

Annabel wasn't troubling to look that far ahead. At one stage she almost cornered the rabbit, only for it to slip away again. By this time they had pursued it across a field, through a hedge – easy for the rabbit, but for Annabel and Kate at the cost of many scratches – across another field and under a barbed wire fence.

All the while Annabel had been crying such things as 'Bunny . . . here, Bun . . . it's all right, nothing to worry about . . . we're friends . . . Bun-Bun, here, boy!'

It came to rest heaving and terrified and Annabel, unwilling to frighten it still further, tried to coax it with sucking noises, stepping gradually closer. Kate stood back and left her to it. Then the rabbit suddenly found a new lease of life and dodged away again, under another wire fence. But it was its last burst.

It made towards a group of buildings lying on the very edge of the dunes and finally came to a stop near the wall of one of them, a big old red brick barn. When Annabel approached it watched her but made no move, seeming to be mesmerized, and allowed itself to be gently picked up without protest. It appeared indeed to have become quite apathetic.

'Oh, Kate, it's in shock,' whispered Annabel, nursing it tenderly. 'It's shivering and its little heart's beating so fast. Oh, and look. Kate – look at its leg. It's all grazed and I'm sure it's broken.'

The foreleg hung limp and apparently useless.

'At least there are some houses here,' panted Kate, who was still recovering. 'We'll be able to get some help.' She herself was grazed, scratched and stung by various plants and insects. She would have weakened and given up long ago if it hadn't been for Annabel, just supposing she'd had the strength to start in the first place, that is.

They looked about them. They were in a tiny hamlet of what appeared to be a farmhouse, a couple of what would once have been labourers' cottages and some barns.

'Let's knock at a door,' said Annabel, making for the nearest cottage. Then they both noticed something.

The cottage's little garden was untended and overgrown and the downstairs windows were boarded up. More than that, as they looked about them they saw that the other houses were in the same condition. The whole hamlet was empty and derelict. Even more than that, however, the farmhouse was partly in ruins and so was one of the barns. The place looked, as Kate's mother sometimes used to say about her bedroom, as if it had been hit by a bomb. Or, in this case, several bombs.

'There's nobody here, Kate,' said Annabel, dismayed. 'What can we do?'

As their attention, which for some time had been focused exclusively on the rabbit, now turned to their surroundings in general they noticed that the narrow road which ran through the hamlet and continued along the foot of the dunes was broken and pot-holed and apparently long disused. They became conscious, too, that the stillness had been broken by a screaming sound in the sky, some way off over the sea but approaching fast.

The screaming became rapidly thunderous and was apparently aimed straight at them. With simultaneous realization they both flung themselves down, Annabel cradling the rabbit protectively beneath her, and covered their ears. As the aircraft flashed overhead and away back over the sea again with a final triumphant thunder-roll they heard the bombs go off in its wake.

2

There were two of them and from the noise Kate assumed they must have exploded just behind the barn by which they had been standing but when she got on to her knees and looked round she saw that the spouts of smoke were rising some distance away on the other side of the dunes, presumably on the beach. She was trembling.

'Oh, Annabel,' she gulped, speaking the first thought that came into her mind, 'we must be trespassing.'

Annabel was rising to her feet, looking affronted.

'Trespassing or not,' she cried, 'this is pretty high-handed.'

'Get down!' shrieked Kate. 'There's another one.'

An identical screaming, approaching from the same direction, was to be heard.

Instead of following Kate's example and flinging herself flat again, however, Annabel snatched a white handkerchief from her pocket. Holding the rabbit tenderly to her with her left hand she started to dance and caper about waving the handkerchief in the air with her right.

To Kate's profound astonishment and relief someone must have seen her for although the aeroplane thundered overhead and turned away over the sea again just as the first one had done, no bombs fell from it and instead of disappearing it came back and proceeded to circle lazily.

Kate scrambled to her feet feeling battered.

'Let's go, Annabel,' she said, urgently.

Annabel, who had done no more than cower a little when the second aircraft had passed over, put the handkerchief back in her pocket.

'We can't go yet, Kate,' she said. 'We've got to do something about poor little Bun-Buns here.' She snuggled him to her. 'Was 'oo frightened then by those horrid noisy aeroplanes?'

'But, Annabel, there's nobody here –'

'There might be water in one of the houses. If the taps are working we can at least bathe his leg.'

'*Annabel –!*'

Annabel was walking towards the cottage with the boarded-up downstairs windows. It had become very noisy overhead and, glancing up, Kate saw that there were now three aircraft circling at different levels. Annabel tried the handle of the door.

'Oh, good. It's open. Come on, Kate. And stop

bothering about those aeroplanes. We've arranged a truce, haven't we? Isn't that what white flags are for?'

With difficulty, Kate wrenched her gaze from the aeroplanes. The door gave straight on to a room from which rose a narrow staircase. It was empty of furnishings, dark, dank and decaying. She was, reluctantly, about to follow Annabel inside when she heard a new engine noise and, looking round, saw that an open-topped army field car was roaring and bouncing very fast along the little pot-holed road towards them. It stopped abruptly outside the cottage.

An exceedingly tall, lean soldier with red bits on his uniform was sitting beside the driver. His long, lean, crisply-moustached face bore the autocratic look of one accustomed to instant obedience.

'What do you think you're doing here?' he roared. 'You're on a range. Could have been killed. Didn't you see the red flag and warning notices?'

'I'm sorry,' said Annabel, 'but we didn't, did we, Kate. We were very busy chasing this rabbit because –'

'Well, get off it. Get in the back and we'll drop you off.'

'– because he's hurt his leg and he's suffering from shock and –' Annabel's tone became reproachful – 'those aeroplanes didn't help.'

The Brigadier, for it was a Brigadier, climbed laboriously down from the car and held the door open.

'Would you please get in   he said, curtly. 'We have an exercise to get on with.

'I'm so glad you've come, though,' said Annabel. 'You've got doctors in the army, haven't you.' She looked at him with winsome appeal.

He was holding a stick which he started tapping against his leg. His tone became biting.

'This,' he said, 'is a NATO combined exercise. Aircraft are waiting patiently to bomb the place. Assault craft are standing by offshore eager for the signal to come in and attack. Some of these men are our allies, travelled from far and wide to be here today. You are holding them all up. Does that mean nothing to you?'

'Imagine,' said Annabel, piteously, 'if he were *your* pet.'

'Sergeant,' said the Brigadier, 'would you go and bring those girls here?'

'Yessir,' said the driver. He started getting out.

Annabel became mutinous. She glanced behind the door. There were two bolts on it.

'I warn you,' she shouted suddenly, 'we are not leaving here till we know this rabbit's all right. This is an errand of mercy which comes before everything else. It's an international convention. Isn't it, Kate?'

She pulled Kate inside, slammed the door and hurled both bolts over. The door was solid, the bolts huge. She rattled up the stairs and Kate, bemused, followed her into a cobwebby bedroom. Annabel was already banging at a window which was sticking.

It flew open in a cloud of woodworm dust and Annabel thrust her head out. The Brigadier was still standing by his vehicle, looking up with the same expression on his face that Kate felt must be on hers.

'We mean what we say,' shouted Annabel. 'Don't we, Kate? Don't we, Bun-Buns?' She hauled the window to again.

The Brigadier carried on staring at the window for a long moment. Then he sighed. He had reached his present high position at an early age by being a realist.

'Sergeant,' he said, 'tell the assault craft to continue

standing by. Ask the RAF if they would kindly carry on circling for a little longer and our apologies if they get dizzy. And get the nearest Medical Officer here. At the double. Or, better still, by helicopter.'

The service couldn't have been better. The rabbit was lifted off in the helicopter only minutes later accompanied by Annabel and Kate to, as Annabel said, hold his paw. The MO, who was very charming and apologized for not being a vet, treated it on board. He cleaned the leg then felt around it, watching the way the rabbit behaved while he did so and pronounced it as almost certainly a sprain rather than a break, though he advised them to get a vet to look at it as soon as possible. In the meantime he put a pressure bandage on it over cotton wool.

The helicopter then touched down in the field just by where they had left their bicycles and Annabel and Kate and the rabbit prepared to get out.

'Thank you very much,' Annabel shouted above the noise. 'And Bun-Bun wants to thank you, too, don't you, Bun-Bun. He looks so much happier now, doesn't he. Look at his little nose twitching. It's a pity we can't thank – I don't know his name – is he your boss? – he has red bits on his uniform.'

'The Brigadier.'

'If you see him would you give him a message?'

'It's unlikely I will but you never know.'

'If you do, say, "Bun-Bun loves you."'

They rode back down the lane on their bikes, the rabbit's head sticking out of Annabel's saddlebag, getting used to the silence. It was broken after a few moments by the now distant sound of an aircraft screaming in from the sea followed by two explosions. The exercise had begun again.

*

Kate's grandparents seemed quite thrilled to learn they were going to be looking after a rabbit for a little while until it could be returned to the wild, and Grandad told a story about an oil-polluted seabird he had once saved. Gran insisted on being the one to take the rabbit to the vet, whose diagnosis agreed perfectly with that of the MO.

Annabel didn't bother to go into long explanations of how the injury had come to be dealt with so expertly for she felt that would merely be unnecessarily worrying for them. She just told them that she and Kate had happened to meet a kindly Brigadier who had arranged for a Medical Officer to help out.

Gran said this just went to show what she had always maintained; that our fighting services were not only the most marvellously brave and efficient in the world but the kindest-hearted, too.

In the evening, Kate's mother rang up to see how they were enjoying themselves and when she'd finished talking, Kate's father came on the line.

'Not drowned yet, then?' he asked, with nervous jollity.

'Not so far, Dad.'

'Not run over or stung by a jellyfish?'

'No.'

'Not fallen off anything?'

'Absolutely nothing.'

'Not even a runaway donkey?'

'Haven't been on any donkeys.'

'Keep it up. That's what we want, isn't it. A nice, quiet, uneventful holiday.'

After putting the phone down, Kate glanced into the sitting-room where Annabel was deep in conversation with her grandparents, with whom she was getting on extremely well. Kate decided to go outside and have another look at the rabbit.

It was recuperating in a wire pen in the back garden and it looked very contented, as well it might. Its nose was twitching cheerfully.

'You are a very lucky rabbit,' Kate told it. 'If I were a rabbit and I had a vision that I was going to be knocked over by a bike and sprain my leg there's just one place in the world where I'd hope to be when it happened. And that's right in front of my friend, Annabel.

'Because I know she'd see me all right.'

Also by Alan Davidson

A FRIEND LIKE ANNABEL

Thirteen-year-old Annabel Fidelity Bunce is considered by many of her fellow pupils in 3G at Lord Willoughby's School to be off her head, and warily tolerated by teachers and other adults of the town, and these five riotously funny, wickedly observant stories prove that with a friend like Annabel, life is certainly never dull.

JUST LIKE ANNABEL

Taking sides with a bored donkey against Mrs da Susa and Mrs Stringer, pillars of Addendon, Annabel and Kate are soon on the trail of the Franks-Walters enigma. With her innocent but exasperating persistence. Annabel discovers that all is not as it appears at Addendon Court! And in the second of these hilarious stories, Annabel inexplicably adopts a 'new attitude' to life.

EVEN MORE LIKE ANNABEL

'There'll be a reign of terror,' Annabel predicts when the repellent Julia Channing is appointed Monitor of the Band Room. And apparently there is! To fight TYRANNY and INJUSTICE, the SILENT THREE, picture strip heroines in an old comic, must rise again. And in the second of these two very funny stories, Annabel plays a central role in Addendon Town Council's spectacular television début.

Some other Puffins

FIRST TERM AT TREBIZON
Anne Digby

At last – a new series of boarding school stories to delight a new generation of readers. In this first story, Rebecca Mason is plunged into life at Trebizon, a famous school for girls. Lonely, afraid and anxious to prove herself, she determines to write something that will be accepted for publication in the special jubilee edition of the school magazine, but the piece that appears is not the one she intended . . .

BOSS OF THE POOL
Robin Klein

The last thing Shelley wanted was to have to spend her evenings at the hostel when all her friends were going away for the summer holidays – all because her mother, who worked there, wouldn't let her stay in the house on her own. Then to her horror, mentally handicapped Ben attaches himself to her from the start and although he's terrified of the pool, he comes to watch her swimming. Despite herself, Shelley begins to help him overcome his fear.

ROB'S PLACE
John Rowe Townsend

Everyone Rob cares for is deserting him: first his dad left, then his best friend, and even his mum hasn't time for him now she has a new husband and baby. Just when he thinks he's got a special friend in Mike, it turns out that he's leaving too. But it's through Mike that Rob learns how to escape from his everyday life – he discovers a fantastic place which is all his own and where he is master. But can he control his fantasy or will his Paradise become a nightmare?

THE BANGERS AND CHIPS EXPLOSION
Brough Girling

When the new cooks arrive in school everyone is delighted, particularly Billy Baxter and his chipaholic friends – every day there are chips on the menu, as many chips as you can eat! But down in the kitchen a terrible plot is brewing – these are no ordinary cooks and they are after much more than second helpings. Only Mrs Perkins, the school secretary, smells something fishy and sets out to investigate.

WILL THE REAL GERTRUDE HOLLINGS PLEASE STAND UP?
Sheila Greenwald

Gertrude is in a bad way. She's a bit slow at school but everyone thinks she's dumb and her teachers call her 'Learning Disabled' behind her back. As if this isn't enough, her parents go off on a business trip leaving her with her aunt and uncle and her obnoxious cousin Albert – a 'superachiever'. Gertrude is determined to win Perfect Prize-winning Albert's respect by whatever means it takes . . .

MAGGIE AND ME
Ted Staunton

Maggie is the undisputed Greenapple Street Genius – and Cyril is her partner. Maggie's always got some brilliant plan, and Cyril inevitably has to help her. Whether it's getting back at the school bully or swapping places for piano lessons, these best friends are always having adventures. Poor Cyril! Life without Maggie would be an awful lot easier, but it would be much more boring. What would he do if she moved away?

WOOF!
Allan Ahlberg

Eric is a perfectly ordinary boy. Perfectly ordinary, that is, until the night when, safely tucked up in bed, he slowly turns into a dog! Fritz Wegner's drawings superbly illustrate this funny and exciting story.

VERA PRATT AND THE FALSE MOUSTACHES
Brough Girling

There were times when Wally Pratt wished his mum was more ordinary and not the fanatic mechanic she was, but when he and his friends find themselves caught up in a real 'cops and robbers' affair, he is more than glad to have his mum, Vera, to help them.

SADDLEBOTTOM
Dick King-Smith

Hilarious adventures of a Wessex Saddleback pig whose white saddle is in the wrong place, to the chagrin of his mother.